WHERE THE LITTLE BIRDS GO

B. CELESTE

WHERE
THE
LITTLE
BIRDS
GO

Where the Little Birds Go

This is a work of fiction. Names, characters, businesses, places, events and incidents are either the products of the author's imagination or used in a fictitious manner. Any resemblance to actual persons, living or dead, or actual events is purely coincidental.

Cover Artist: RBA Designs

Formatting: Micalea Smeltzer

Published by: B. Celeste

ALSO BY B. CELESTE

The Truth about Heartbreak
The Truth about Tomorrow
The Truth about Us
Underneath the Sycamore Tree

playlist

"Hollywood's Bleeding" – Post Malone
"Lose You to Love Me" – Selena Gomez
"Picture" – Kid Rock ft. Cheryl Crow
"Consequences" – Camila Cabello
"Circles" – Post Malone
"Lover" – Taylor Swift
"It Will Rain" – Bruno Mars
"Stay With Me" – Sam Smith

To the dreamers

where the little birds go

b. celeste

prologue

KINLEY / Present

I never expected him to come crashing back into my life. Without warning, without a single clue, I was face to face with my greatest weakness. Nobody knew that I was already familiar with the silver-eyed charmer whose face encompassed every magazine, newsstand, and Hollywood tabloid cover across the country.

Before Corbin Callum became America's biggest star, he was just the new kid in the middle of nowhere. I knew all his secrets from the start—where he got the scar on his right eyebrow, why he has two black tally marks tattooed on his left pec, and who he lost his virginity to. None of that is information I gathered from the press or pieced together by rumors.

Long before we dove headfirst into the industries we've dreamed of being big figures in, we made a pact that we'd never leave each other behind. But our aspirations were larger than the old versions of ourselves that thought everything would remain the same. We couldn't keep up the charade, pretending to be the teenagers who had the world at their feet.

Once upon a time, I was his.

Before the fame.

Before the money.

Before *her*.

For a long time, I accepted that we'd never see each other again. But here we are.

He meets my eyes and grins.

"Hey, Little Bird."

one

CORBIN / Present

I'VE OFFICIALLY LOST it at twenty-eight. Despite the half-naked woman sporting nothing but a white t-shirt and black panties in front of me, I'm staring at a fully clothed one through distorted glass. The way her chestnut hair flows down her back as she laughs at something somebody in front of her says has me harder than the scrap of lace over a tan pert ass five feet away. I know the husky laugh well. I've even been the cause of it a time or two.

But that was before.

Suddenly, I'm not picturing the blonde in my

clothes. I'm picturing a familiar brunette with a curvy body under a thin sheet of my favorite worn cotton. A small birthmark in the shape of a heart would peek out from the fabric on her inner thigh, where I'd be able to trace it with my finger.

The brunette isn't in front of me though. She's too busy talking to world renown Tyler Buchannan as he flirts his way into her good graces in hopes that'll lead to a few glasses of wine and a strip show in the penthouse he rented.

Unbeknownst to him, she doesn't drink. At least, she didn't. I guess that could have changed over the past ten years. I'd be a fucking fool to think nothing else has.

The front of my slacks gets too tight for comfort as my head conjures old memories of bare skin under my old AC/DC sweatshirt. That birthmark likes to make its appearance in the back of my mind more times than not, and I can still feel the sensation of smooth skin under my fingertips like it was yesterday.

"My, my," a sultry voice purrs.

Slowly, my eyes meet a pair of blue ones staring down at the hard dick tenting my pants. Adjusting myself with no shame, I settle into the chair I've been in for the past ten minutes.

"Is that for me?" Olivia asks, shooting me the same wicked grin she gave me the first day we ever worked together. I like Olivia Davies. She's always easy to work with, and certainly not bad on the eyes. She referred to herself as Hitler's wet dream once, which didn't go over well with the press we were doing interviews with. I cracked up, and both our managers scolded us for the shitshow we created.

"Don't flatter yourself." Stretching my legs out and crossing my arms over my chest, I nod toward the free chair beside me. "I wasn't thinking about you."

I'm sure she rolls her eyes as she takes a seat, sitting sideways on the chair and using the back as an armrest. "I'm sure. You were thinking about Lena, right? Honestly, I would be too. I can admit when I have a girl crush. She gives me a lady boner."

I find my gaze locked on chestnut hair again, her facial features cracked from the thick decorated glass separating us. "Uh ... what?"

"Lena," Liv repeats, snorting out an amused laugh. "Your wife?"

I roll my shoulders back and force myself to look around the kitchen. Anything but the woman outside it. Everything here looks shiny, expensive, and new. The cabinets are dark wood, the countertops white granite, and the appliances all featuring the best of the best with brands I'm sure are helping fund the project through sponsorships.

"Yeah."

Except that's a lie. The only woman who should get me this hard with a single memory *should* be my wife.

5

Unfortunately for me, that isn't the five-seven figure walking alongside Buchannan as he gives her a tour.

Things with Lena aren't what they seem. We spend far more time apart than together, so it's practically like being single with limitations. I have a better relationship with my right hand than I do with the woman I made vows to.

"Definitely thinking about my wife."

Liv nudges my foot with hers and tips her chin toward the side of the set. "What do you think Buchannan and Kinley are talking about? I doubt his new girlfriend is a fan of her books, so I'm sure it isn't that. I'm not sure she can even read."

Chuckling over the sad but true knock at the ditzy redhead who Buchannan is stringing along for the time being, I shake my head. "They're probably going over expectations of the film."

You know, if expectations were telling her where his hotel is and what number is on the door. I've worked with Buchannan before, and know his reputation. Women as gorgeous as Kinley Thomas can't be ignored by men with prying eyes like him.

Olivia full on cackles now. "Yeah, sure. I thought writers were, like, introverted hermits. You know, kinda smelly and sensitive to sunlight."

I don't want to tell Liv that Kinley has never fit the stereotypical author role. That would mean I know her, and that's far from true at this point. Once upon a time,

I knew that she loved Twizzlers, action movies, and teaching herself origami using notes from class. She hated mayonnaise, movies where animals get neglected, and when people called her anything but her full name. It's why part of me thought I was breaking the ice by using an old nickname only I ever called her. It was our thing.

Little Bird.

Turns out, I was wrong.

"Well?" Liv presses.

"Hmm?"

"What's your opinion on Kinley?"

That's a loaded question.

Besides the film industry, my oldest fascination has been the shy girl who preferred journaling on her own over going out with friends. She has a scar on her left cheek from when her family's chow-chow bit her. Once she tried covering it up with makeup, but it was the dead of summer and the shit melted off and made it more pronounced. Any flaw she thought she had was my favorite part of her—scars, aversion to people, and all.

"She seems like the kind of woman who won't fall for Buchannan's tricks," is what I opt to settle with after thinking on it for too long.

She laughs, letting it go.

"We're filming in two," Buchannan yells from his chair at the other end of the set. Next to him is Kinley's

7

seat, which is placed a little too close to his. I tell myself it wasn't her who put the chair there, but it doesn't ease the irrational irritation bubbling under my skin.

Liv gets up and puts the chair back how she found it, shooting me a wink before swaying her hips provocatively where she's supposed to start the scene by the counter. I roll my eyes at her as I settle on the chair as cued, resting one arm on the edge of the table while watching her closely. My legs are spread, my teeth are digging into my bottom lip, and I study her like I studied Kinley Thomas before I fucked everything up.

"And, action!"

Olivia grabs a wine glass and glances over at me. Her eyes are lust-filled as they scan down my body, landing on the slight bulge beneath my zipper.

"I have a feeling you're going to be a bad influence," she says, delivering her line as she begins filling her glass with Pinot Noir.

Swiping my bottom lip with my thumb, I shift in the seat and stare at her exposed ass. "I don't think you have a problem with that."

She fights off a grin. "There's a special place in hell for people like us, you know."

"People in love?"

She lifts the glass to her lips. "Cheaters."

two

Kinley / Present

THE BLENDED MIXTURE of red and yellow across the California skyline is dulled by the glow of skyscrapers lining the distance. Heart racing as I take another step further onto the tenth-story balcony attached to my hotel room, I absorb the noise of a nightlife I'm foreign to. For the first time in years, I think about how much I miss the middle of nowhere I grew up in.

Closing the outer door, I back into the main room of the prestigious suite that Tyler Buchannan set me up with. Everything is white, modern, and sleek—far from the odd mixture of farmhouse-meets-contemporary that litters my three-bedroom townhome in Upstate New York.

When the opportunity came, I couldn't distance myself from the place I called home for twenty years. How many times had I told everyone I'd get out of Lincoln? Move? Go somewhere farm animals didn't outnumber humans? Yet, the house I purchased almost four years ago is mere hours away from the family I thought I'd long since said goodbye to.

A soft knock at the door has my brows pinching, especially when my name is called following room service that I never ordered. Though I considered taking advantage of the free food Buchannan offered me on the movie's expense, my stomach has been too full of eerily familiar flutters since seeing Corbin Callum parading around set like he owned it.

The annoying thing is, he did.

He is the epitome of Ryker Evans.

Sex appeal.

Confident.

A vulnerability so few people see.

Tugging on the hem of the AC/DC sweatshirt that I slipped on over my pajama pants, I look through the peephole at the pepper-haired man in hotel uniform. My outfit isn't very public friendly, not that I neces-sarily care about what strangers think of me. But the sweatshirt is a well-worn keepsake that I hate myself for wearing. I don't remember packing it, but the second my eyes landed on the holey fabric and faded letters, the anxiety I felt since landing in California eased.

The hotel worker greets me again as I open the door, gesturing toward the tray on the cart between us. Whatever rests under the serving tray smells delicious, but it doesn't lessen my confusion.

"I think there's been a mistake," I offer, giving him a grateful smile. "It smells amazing, but I didn't order anything."

The man shakes his head. "No mistake, ma'am. It was called in for you to be delivered straight to your room."

I blink. "By...?"

He just smiles. "I'm only the delivery man, ma'am. Somebody will come by to collect the tray outside your room when you're finished. Enjoy your dinner."

Dismissed, I accept the tray and close the door behind me with a murmured *thank you*. The faint smell of salt and something familiar wafts into the air, leaving my curiosity piquing. Setting the silver on the table closest to me, I take off the lid and stare at what lays underneath.

When I notice the note sitting beside the burger and fries, I pluck it off and open it. I don't expect to see what's scrawled in decent handwriting across the hotel stationary. My eyes travel to the smaller tray off to the side, still covered with something peeking out of the corner. My fingers hesitantly lift the lid, freezing when the packaged plastic of Twizzlers appears.

Leaning my hip against the table, my fingers smooth over the inked letters.

We'll keep making the same mistakes because we never want to learn.
-Ryker

I REMEMBER READING those very words a thousand times after I received the script from the screenwriter. They were straight from my book—a sentence I'd debated on deleting countless times because they'd been a truth I hadn't wanted to accept.

Corbin Callum is a mistake I'll keep making because I'm not ready to learn from him yet. All of the pain that comes from old memories should turn me away for good, but something holds me back from cutting the string that ties me to those silver eyes I looked directly into when I said I loved him back then.

The sad part is, I'd tell him again if I thought it'd make a difference.

three

KINLEY / 16

FROM THE CORNER of my eye, I notice a boy with messy brown hair drop into a seat outside of the principal's office. As if he can feel me staring, he turns and locks eyes with me through the glass that separates us. He's got one earbud in his ear, the other dangling freely against his shoulder, and his legs spread like he's prepared to stay a while.

I don't recognize him, and I would. Not just because Lincoln is a small town with an even smaller school district, but because he's got that look I read about in books. The carefree boyish one that screams charm and trouble. Quirked lips and a challenging gaze—he's daring me to look away.

Adjusting my backpack on my shoulder, I walk into the main office and smile at the secretary. She's typing something a mile a minute with her acrylic nails tapping in a blur of dark red. It seems fitting for the start of fall that's bound to hit central New York in the coming weeks. The leaves haven't started changing, but the temperature has dropped.

Mrs. Lewis, the white-haired secretary, tells me she'll be just a second. Knowing her, she's got something due in a matter of minutes. She loves playing Bejeweled Blitz on her phone all day until deadlines near. Then she'll ignore everybody until her work is done.

It gives me time to study the new kid. I try doing it subtly because his eyes are still pointed in my direction. My fingers dig through the candy bowl, searching absently for something to nibble on despite it being eight in the morning. Through my lashes, I peek at the boy whose lips are twitching upward at me.

Shifting from one foot to the other, I glance down at my dirtied combat boots. I found them at a thrift store in town, practically new. One of the laces is coming undone, so I drop down and redo them. The new kid is wearing a pair of black ones like mine that look shiny and new. They match his black ensemble—black jeans and black shirt with white words faded across his chest like he's owned it a while. His leg is bouncing, and I wonder if it's to the music he's listening to or impatience.

Standing back up, I move loose pieces of hair behind my ear. The color is usually brown, but I asked Mom to help me dye it before the new school year started. Now I have auburn and caramel highlights that makes my hair look anything but brunette.

When my gaze wanders back over to where the boy sits, we lock eyes until I flush under his direct stare. He doesn't seem ashamed to be openly gawking at me like I am him. That's when I notice how unnerving his eyes are. They aren't just any normal gray, but a striking shade of silver. From here, the light hitting the mischievous gleam of the hues turns them almost white.

Grandma told me once that you can tell a person is bad news by the way they smile. *It's the way their lips curve, Kinley. It's even worse if they have a twinkle in their eye.*

And this kid, whoever he is, has the very twinkle Grandma always warned me about. She said she's had decades of experience, making her an expert on who to avoid. Yet, my interest is piqued by the boy sitting across the room from me. The way he's perched in the chair is both casual and not, like he knows he needs to be here, but doesn't want to be. *Who are you, New Kid?*

Wetting my dry, chapped lips, I examine the thin layer of dust on Mrs. Lewis's fake plant. I'm half tempted to grab a tissue and wipe it off, but I force my hands to remain at my sides.

"Um, Mrs. Lewis?" The clock on the wall shows that homeroom is almost over, which means I'll be late to first period if she doesn't tell me why I was called down here.

"Just one more moment, dear."

Internally sighing, I plop down into the closest seat. It's an uncomfortable plastic chair that belongs in the elementary wing, but I don't complain too much because it puts distance between me and the boy with silver eyes.

For some reason, I feel the need to look up again. I'm not sure why, because there are plenty of other things to look at. Like the new assistant principal who's talking rapidly on the phone in his office. His image is cut off by the busted blinds on the windowed wall, but whoever he's speaking to is getting an earful.

New Kid shifts in his seat when he catches me watching him. "You just going to stare or do you plan on saying something?"

My eyes widen. "Uh…"

He chuckles and reaches for his pocket, pulling out his phone. After a few seconds, his music stops, and the room is bathed in silence. From a distance, I hear heels clicking on hard flooring, girls laughing, and a ball dribbling.

"Sorry," I murmur, embarrassment prickling the back of my neck and cheeks.

Shoes scuffing against tile has me looking from the grubby floor to the new kid as he grabs his belongings and moves over to the chair next to me.

He shoots me a wink with eyes that look far more magnetic from up close, especially framed with dark lashes. "I'm always down for a cute girl giving me attention."

Thankfully, I don't need to reply before Mrs. Lewis looks up between him and I. Her signature bright blue eye shadow covers her lids, and there's black mascara smudged under her right eye, magnified by her thick brown glasses.

"Oh, good! You've met Mr. Callum." Her smile is wide and showcases the slightest hint of smeared lipstick on one of her front teeth. I debate on saying something but opt to focus on the name I'm supposed to recognize.

Mrs. Lewis picks up something from the printer beside her and waves it at us. "This is his schedule. You know the drill, Kinley. Locker number and everything is listed by his information on the top. Principal Gilbert just wants you to show him around."

Lips parting in surprise, I chance a quick look at the

new kid. I figured my chances of being summoned to the office weren't severe. I've never been in trouble in my life. Well, not intentionally. I agreed to hold onto a flash drive once for a friend and then got escorted to the office in tears when I found out it had a recorded fight on it that the school was investigating. I broke down as soon as the principal called me in to ask questions. One of the teachers who was helping investigate vouched for my good behavior. It pays to be a teacher's pet I suppose.

New Kid smirks again. "This new school is looking better than my last one already."

His *last* one? Why was there one before this? Military families don't exactly settle into the middle of nowhere. Civilization is at least two hours in any direction—cities, stoplights, businesses don't exist here. Lincoln has more cows than humans, and the only stoplight in the middle of town is usually ignored because it takes too long to change.

That leaves other possibilities. Behavioral ones. I've gotten my fill of becoming friends with all the wrong people since high school started two years ago. My plan now is simple—go to school, get good grades, and get out. I don't want distractions deterring me from graduating a year early and living out my dreams. Especially distractions with silver eyes and an up-to-no-good smile.

New Kid gets up and takes the schedule from Mrs. Lewis, who gives us her toothy smile before dismissing us with her eyes. She has Bejeweled Blitz to get back to.

Sighing, I walk out of the office with the new kid on my heels. His long legs catch up to me quickly, and I feel his gaze on my face. He's taller than me, that much I can tell from my peripheral. Six two? Six three? He reminds me of Justin Fully, who sprouted well past six foot after seventh grade. Except unlike Justin's lanky frame, the new kid has an athletic build that fills him out in a flattering way—like he's involved with sports or physical labor. Some of the farm kids have thick arms they like to show off when the school year starts, especially the tans that color them until the first cold snap hits.

A white earbud hangs out of New Kid's pocket, unwound from the device he stuffed there before chasing after me. He pays it no attention, but it bugs me more than I like to admit. The wires will get all tangled and ruined.

He glances down. "You see anything you're interested in?"

At first, I don't understand what he's getting at, but when he wiggles his eyebrows suggestively my whole face heats up. I keep my gaze pointed at my boots as I walk toward the high school stairwell at the other end of the hall.

New Kid finally falls into step beside me, reaching into his pocket and pulling out his phone. I think he's going to put his music back on and ignore me, but he winds up the buds and lets it drop back into his jeans instead.

"Is black your favorite color or something?" His black jeans are distressed with scuffs and rips along the left leg. I always liked the style, but Dad always makes comments about how pointless they are, especially because they cost so much money for what little material is offered.

"No."

One word, that's all I get.

Clearing my throat, I ask, "Where's your locker listed? I can show you that first."

Instead of answering me, he studies the class photos lining the main hallway. It goes back to when the school merged with the neighboring town's district in 1996. He goes to each one until we're farther from where we need to be.

I blurt, "I don't like the way you walk."

He peels his eyes away from the glass frames and grins at me like I just said something amusing instead of randomly insulting.

"Why don't you like the way I walk?"

We spend a few moments in silence as he saunters back over to me. There's a big watch on his wrist that looks expensive and out of place considering most people our age use their phones to look at the time.

"I just ... don't." The words don't come out easy

when he stares at me like he is. Everything about him screams confidence. I'm the exact opposite.

"Don't be like that, Birdy."

My brows pinch until curiosity has me looking up at him. Mischief dances across his features, the corners of his lips quirked up until dimples pop out on either side of his mouth.

"Don't call me that."

He winks. "Seems appropriate. You're flighty when it comes to answering my questions."

I'm flighty? He ignored me to look at old photos like he'd rather see the evolution of hairstyles, rather than answer a simple question.

He starts walking further down the hall, causing me to try catching up with him. Nothing but the squeal of our shoes against the freshly polished floors fills the silence between us.

I'm prepared to respond when he suddenly stops by the auditorium. One of the double sets of doors is propped open. The janitors are probably cleaning after it was used for the middle school assembly on drug use this morning.

When he starts walking in, I snap out of my train of thought and grab his arm. "What are you doing? You can't go in there."

He rolls his eyes and peeks in. It's nothing special to look at. There are three sections of seating, and a medium sized wooden stage in the front of the room.

Currently, the two sets of black curtains are open, revealing the cobblestone wall that matches the exterior of the school. On the rest of the beige walls are random geometric shapes that match the school's forest green color scheme. We're home of the Spartans.

"They do plays here?" His question is almost lost on me because he's studying the stage contently. It isn't until he looks over his shoulder at me and tips his head toward the room again that I muster an answer.

"Yeah."

They've already started meeting afterschool about the winter play. I heard someone say it's going to be a musical, but for such a small school it's very hush-hush. I'm betting on *Grease*, since that's a fan favorite.

He hums before turning toward me. "Do you participate in them?"

Me? I blink, wondering if he's kidding. Then I remember that he doesn't know me, which means he doesn't know how awkward I am in front of people. "Um ... no."

He tilts his head. "Why not?"

I give him a small shrug. It's really a comfort thing —not a difficult answer. Somehow I don't think that'll be good enough for him though.

"I'm not much into acting, I guess."

There's no guessing about it. The only acting I do is when I come home and tell everyone I had a good day at school. It's a tale I spin to stop my brother from threatening petty people who make fun of me over stupid things like staying quiet or eating alone.

We begin walking again. "What are you into then?" He stops in the middle of the hall, his boots making a horrendous sound against the tile. "Wait, let me guess. You're the bookish type who loses herself in period pieces where the men insult the available women until they inevitably get married because they've always truly loved each other, right?"

I blink. Then blink again. "Did you just describe *Pride and Prejudice*?"

His grin returns. "Unlike you, I happen to love acting. My old school's drama club did a year's worth of Jane Austen adaptations."

"And I assume you always got the lead?"

He doesn't have to tell me with words.

He tells me with his eyes—with his confidence. It radiates off him like his own personal spotlight. I wonder if it gets too hot.

Shaking my head, I fight off the small smile that wants to tilt my lips. If they curve upward, I lose. New Kid can't win.

He steps forward, the tips of his boots nudging the ends of mine. "Come on, Birdy. You know you want to smile."

My brows arch. "I told you not to—"

"Fine," he relents, studying me. My five-foot-seven frame feels puny compared to him. He notices the

B. CELESTE

difference as much as me, looking down to catch my eye. "Little Bird is far better."

My jaw clenches. "I'm not flighty."

He steps back. "Sure you're not."

He's the epitome of Mr. Darcy.

"What am I supposed to call you?"

His eyes flash. "Corbin. Corbin Callum."

four

CORBIN / Present

CRAFT FOOD SERVICE has a few tables set up in the main hall for everyone working on the lot. By lunch, they're all surrounded by scatterings of people talking amongst themselves about industry gossip. I'm not interested in who got implants, who broke up, or who had a mental breakdown.

My feet guide me to the Italian buffet, where salad, pasta, and breadsticks are lined up in a tidy row of steel trays. Stepping to the side of where Kinley places leafy greens on her plate, I grab a breadstick and tear off an end.

"You should use the serving utensils."

Besides a quick hello to save face when introductions were made in front of the entire cast, this is the first voluntary conversation we're having one on one. The last thing I want it to turn into is a half-ass lecture on how to properly utilize buffet style lunches. I want to talk about her. How she's doing. If she's as excited about this film adaptation as much as I am to be part of it.

Grabbing a plate and putting the torn bread onto it, I follow her along the edge of the table and absentmindedly pile food up. "You used to hate Italian."

She stops and finally, *finally* looks at me. Her dark brown eyes don't hold a friendly hue to them though. They're distant round orbs that give me no indication to what she's thinking.

The rest of her is the same, just older than I remember. Her round face is slightly more defined, her cheekbones more prominent, and her lips still full like I used to love. She never wore makeup to emphasize any of the features other girls would kill to have. Like the long dark lashes that flutter whenever she tries to look at me without giving herself away. I recognize her old mannerisms. She used to hate getting caught staring, but like me, she can't quite stop.

Her gaze dips to the piles of dirty dishes off to the side, trying her best to keep the conversation boring. "Why don't they use disposable?" she asks, not directing the question to anyone specific as she walks to a nearby empty table.

My desperation to hold a conversation with her has me jumping on the opportunity. "I think they like to keep staff busy so they're not loitering during shooting. Most of them are happy to do just about anything if it means being near people like us."

Brows arching, she blinks up at me. "I guess you're going to have to explain that to me. Who exactly is 'people like us'?"

Rubbing my lips together, I shift under her scrutinizing gaze. "I just meant, uh ... you know, actors. Celebrities. A lot of the people employed to cook, serve, and clean do it to be part of whatever films are shooting on location."

Picking up her fork, she shakes her head and stabs a chickpea from her salad mix. "I'm kind of relieved. For a minute I thought maybe you'd changed. I'm glad to know you're still an asshole though."

My lips part in surprise. The Kinley I knew rarely swore unless she thought it was justified. She kept to herself to avoid confrontation, never initiated it so bluntly.

She glances from her plate to me. "Did you ever think that maybe the people hired to do those mundane tasks are just happy to have a job? I know this is beyond you, superstar, but people are motivated by money more than fame."

"It's Hollywood," I point out, a little dumbfounded by her quick judgement. "I'm not saying they're not happy to be employed doing some shit job for even shittier pay, but you have to admit some of them are here to ogle us too."

When her fork drops onto her plate with a loud *clink*, I know I'm in for it. Kinley Thomas loves food. Rarely will she stop eating to give anyone a piece of her mind, but I've witnessed it before. Her thoughts build in her head until she's ready to combust and can't hold it in.

"I used to be a dish washer once, remember? The Tryon was my first real job that, yeah, only paid minimum wage. It wasn't fun, the people weren't that great, and the hours sucked. It was work though. Quit talking about the people who do the jobs you think sound awful like they're beneath you."

Swallowing, I try stopping her from standing up. "Kin—"

She grabs her plate. "No."

"I wasn't trying to be an ass."

"It's your default mode," she informs me matter-of-factly. "Sometimes I think you can't help it, especially not now. I mean, I should congratulate you, Corbin." My name on her lips stirs something in me that has been dormant for too long. "You're exactly where you want to be. I know how hard you worked to live out your dreams. Great job. You did it."

Her praise does little for me because the disappoint-ment hanging on every word drowns out the pride I should be reveling in.

She grips the plate a little tighter in her hands, like it's her way of keeping control. "Do you remember when people in Lincoln told us never to forget where we came from? They didn't want us to forget the little people. Well, I haven't forgotten. Have you?"

Not knowing what to say to make this better, we just stand there staring at each other until she chooses to walk away. It's symbolic. She's making the decision now that I made ten years ago.

Dropping my plate onto the table and wincing at the carbs I loaded up on, I kick my feet back and stare over at Kinley's retreating figure. She smiles and waves at someone who calls her name before disappearing around the corner.

"That went well," I murmur to myself.

LENA DASANI IS A BLACK-HAIRED, blue-eyed power-house I never expected to meet. We met through a mutual friend four years ago, when I was invited to a New Year's Eve party. It took one little look, the slightest batting of eyelashes, and a simple brush of the hand before we became attached at the hip.

Being with Lena gave me hope. Despite the press capturing pictures of me with random women before her, I rarely went out or hooked up more than a few times a year. Nothing ever compared to the feeling I got when I was a teenager, no matter how hard I chased to find it again.

I'm getting ready to head to the car that's waiting to take me back to my condo on the outskirts of the city when my phone goes off. Swiping the tip of my tongue across my bottom lip when I see Lena's name on the screen, I clear my throat and pause by my designated trailer.

Holding up a finger at the driver waiting for me by the black Escalade, I press the cell against my ear. "Hey, Lena."

Her soft Greek accent greets me, as I lean back against the cool metal siding. "I haven't heard from you all day. I figured you'd call me during your lunch break like usual."

She's visiting her family in Greece while I spend time filming. It's typical for a quick Skype call while cast gets a meal break since there's a ten-hour time difference between us.

"I didn't have time," I lie, glancing at the clock on my phone. "Isn't it early there? I figured I'd text you before I went to bed that way I didn't wake you."

There's murmuring in the background, her response to whomever soft before she focuses back on me. "I was up early with a friend. And surely you know I'd want more than a text from my husband."

The implication of phone sex that our conversations usually lead to is heavy in her lust-ridden words. It makes my cock twitch in the jeans I changed into right after reshooting the last scene since Buchannan insisted it wasn't up to par with the others. Normally, it'd piss me off to be told my work isn't good enough. Despite the reputation I'm labeled with, I can admit when I'm sucking ass at work. Kinley watching my every move put me on edge, especially following the little one-on-one we had at lunch.

Nothing about what I sent her last night was mentioned all day, and part of me wondered if she even got it. But the persisting avoidance in her lingering gaze every time her eyes found mine between scenes told me she received everything. Her impressive quickness in looking away when I'd catch her watching me told me what I needed to know.

"Callum?" The name snaps me from driving down that dangerous path, making me cringe at the way my own wife refers to me by my last name like the industry does.

"Sorry." I straighten my spine, rolling my shoulders back and try refocusing. "I miss you. I hope you know that."

Marriage never used to be in my scope of vision when I was younger. Having a thriving career and traveling were the only two things my one-tracked mind could focus on. Every time an opportunity would arise to go out, I'd find excuses to stay in. Work would get me out of most situations where friends would try setting me up, but there were a few women I let in as welcome distractions.

By the time I met Lena, I'd made a name for myself across the world. No longer was I Corbin Callum from small town New York. My year spent in Lincoln only cemented my drive that got me to become Callum— America's leading bad boy. Honestly, the title is laughable. Minus an altercation I'd gotten into with some paparazzi outside a hotel I'd been staying at who accused me of buying my way into a role I'd worked my ass off to get, I'd stayed clean in the media. I was known to drink a little too much depending on my moods, but besides pictures of me drinking at parties or smoking on sets if I have a shitty day, there's not much else people can get from me.

I never stop people from calling me Callum because it beats them highlighting my real name for research purposes. I'm sure plenty of people have dug up pieces of my past with a basic Google search, but I made sure to clean up anything involving Lincoln so my new life wouldn't intercept with my old one.

"I miss you too, baby." She purrs the words that would undoubtedly lead to phone sex on any other day. The premise has me semi-hard, yet my mood is anything but ready to jerk off in the back of the car, much less in the condo we occasionally share.

Rubbing my neck, I say, "Listen, Len, I need to get back home and try getting some rest. It's an early call tomorrow morning. We'll be shooting pretty late too."

There's a pregnant pause between us that makes me flinch. "Okay."

"I love you."

Someone speaks to her from the other end of the line—a cousin probably. One of her best friends growing up was Silas, who's only a year older than her. He was the one person I could talk to and understand without Lena having to translate when I visited her family on the island.

"Call me when you have time," is her monotone response before the line cuts off.

Clicking my tongue and staring at the *call ended* message on the screen, I shove the cell into my pocket and make my way to the car. There are only a few vehicles in the lot compared to the packed spaces earlier.

Olivia left after talking to a few of our co-stars who seemed excited to begin filming more of their parts tomorrow. Today was a few essential scenes between Olivia and I, including a racier make out session that will lead to the first sex scene we're expected to shoot bright and early tomorrow morning.

Her departing words for me were, *try not to get too hard for me. I don't need you poking an eye out.*

Snorting as I settle into the backseat, I pull out my phone while we start out of the lot onto the busy street.

I know it'll take time getting home because the nightlife rush hour is insane. My fingers scroll through a few messages from friends before I find myself on Facebook typing the last name I should be interested in searching.

Kinley blocked me on social media months after I left Lincoln. I don't blame her after I promised to keep in touch and never followed through. It was never intentional to hurt her, but life got busy when the jobs started picking up. My time became limited to filming, working out, and resting like my new manager and trainer suggested. I began doing everything in my power to be the actor that people wanted to hire without a second thought. Lincoln became a distant memory, but Kinley never did even if she thought so. How could she not? By the time I worked up the guts to reach out, her number didn't work.

It was around a year ago when news broke about the film that I found a mutual friend's post congratulating her on an interview she did with Entertainment Daily. Temptation had me clicking her name before spending hours going through the life she cut me off from. Everything she posted since shutting me out became my addiction in the little free time I had. Dating updates made me scowl, book accomplishments made me smile, and pictures made my heart tug a little tighter in my chest like it did back in high school.

Pausing when I see a selfie she took with Olivia and a few other cast members on set today, I study the background to figure out when it was taken. I never saw them stop and take pictures together, and I was on set a majority of the day. I'm full on glaring when I see a few more of the sets and a picture someone took of her and Buchannan talking off to the side of the bedroom they put together for tomorrow's scenes.

"What the fuck is this?" I growl aloud.

"Sir?"

Wincing, I look up at the driver who's looking at me through the rearview. "Sorry. Just something I saw online."

He replies with a simple nod before returning his eyes to the traffic we're stuck in.

Kinley went out of her way to avoid taking a picture with me. When I click through the comments and read them, I notice a few people ask where I am. Her reply? *He was busy.*

Nose flaring, I'm half-tempted to comment just to see what she'll say. The post is public, so it wouldn't be impossible. However, my fake name and passive aggressive remark would probably give me away. My old account had to be deactivated and then deleted when people were hacking into it after my career took off. The alias I use on the downlow is for keeping up with friends and family ... and occasionally checking in on Kinley.

Turning my phone off, I stare out the window. They're tinted, so I can people watch without any chaos ensuing. I learned the hard way what some fans will do for a quick picture. The last thing I want is to be trapped in backed up traffic that'll take a police escort to get me out of just to see my condo before dawn.

"Want any music on, sir?"

I should probably learn the guy's name since he was assigned to me for the duration of shooting. It'd probably make Kinley think of me better since our last conversation didn't end well. For some reason though, I'm unable to conjure the simple question.

So all I say is, "No, thank you."

five

KINLEY / Present

MY LEG BOUNCES as I watch the crew put finishing touches on the set. The vases of artificial flowers lining the dark brown dresser are bright colors that liven up the otherwise plain room, which is exactly what I imagined for Beck. Her simplicity shows in every scene that showcases her home, rivaling the complicated nature of her relationship with Ryker.

Biting down on another Twizzler from my seat, my eyes scope out the remaining sets nearby. Everything they put together exceeds my expectations. Half the furnished rooms make me envy my own décor at home, and they added the slightest details that made Beck and Ryker who they are—the wine, the pictures on the walls, the way Beck has to have every little detail perfected even though Ryker teases her about it.

There's a playfulness between the two that makes you root for them despite knowing you shouldn't. When my eyes lock on a picture of Olivia and Corbin off to the side, I hop off my chair and walk over to the display of frames lining the shelf near the bed.

Each one is layered with little knick-knacks and images of different people—some who I met already over the past few days, and some I haven't seen at all. My fingers trail along the edge of the smooth espresso-colored wood when I stop dead in my tracks at one of the silver frames at the end.

"What the h—"

"I think it fits well," a familiar voice says from close behind me.

Turning abruptly with the picture in hand, I hold it up between us. "How did they get this picture, Corbin?"

Corbin's smile doesn't waver when the cold tone of my voice ices the room. "Come on, Little—" My death glare stops him. "—*Kinley*. It's a cute photo. Plus, a lot of authors have little cameo's in the movies based on their books."

Nostrils flaring, I shake the frame containing an awkward photo taken by Corbin's mom a few days after my seventeenth birthday. My hair is in a messy bun, my smile is too big, too fake, and I'm pretty sure I'm looking at Corbin who was making faces behind his mother's back. At that point, our friendship-turned-more was rocky and awkward.

"Do I look like Stan Lee?" I hiss, gripping the picture tighter in my grasp. "It doesn't even make sense. It's a nice gesture, but it shouldn't be here. It doesn't go with the others."

Humor dances in Corbin's eyes, making them the stupid shade of white I used to get weak-kneed over. "People have pictures of friends in their houses. It fits just fine."

Closing my eyes, I take a deep breath to calm myself down. "How did they get it?"

When he doesn't answer, I open my eyes and narrow them at a face I told myself to keep my distance from. His lips draw in, in a telltale sign of guilt. It's a silent admittance, but one I know all too well.

I've studied that look plenty of times since he kissed me goodbye after his graduation party. I didn't know it at the time, but he had the same expression on his face. How long had he known what his life would turn out to be? How long did he know I wouldn't be in it?

Tears want to well in my eyes, but I force them back

behind the wall I've built. It's cracked and leaking, but strong enough to hold the emotions that want to burst from the seams. Too many defenses have failed me before, and this is all I have—fake hatred mixed with real anger. A deadly combination when silver eyes see right through the façade.

"I just suggested they get a picture or two to display around set," he finally admits, lifting his shoulders in an easy shrug. "They thought it was a great idea and figured you'd appreciate the random cameos. You know, mixing real with fiction."

I shake my head and place the frame back where I found it, staring at the smile young me is casting to young Corbin.

"Why Corbin?" I ask quietly. When he doesn't answer, I gesture around us. "Why Ryker? Why this movie? Why *now*?"

His lips part, but nothing comes out.

I take the Twizzlers out from the bag hanging on my shoulder and slam them into his chest. Only a few are missing since he gave them to me. I couldn't get myself to accept the gift, but the sugar was exactly what I needed when my nerves got the better of me this morning.

"Why the candy?" It comes out a broken whisper that has his lips curving down. "You shouldn't have bothered. With the food, the candy, the note. *The note.* There's no point, so why?"

He takes a step forward despite the little room between us already. The tips of his expensive looking shined black shoes tap my basic heeled wedges that I got from the clearance rack at Target. Nothing about my floral wrap dress screams money or class like the button-down white shirt tucked into belted black dress pants does on his slim frame. I know Ryker's signature look—the rolled sleeves, the three top buttons undone, and the messy bedroom hair.

I also know Corbin Callum even though I wish I didn't. He dresses to impress. To play any part. And he plays it well, just like he always has.

The best friend.

The loving boyfriend.

The heartbreaker.

"There's always a point," he tells me quietly, keeping his hands tucked into his pockets. His gravelly tone has the power to make me come undone, and I hate it. "It's an apology, for one."

Now I'm rolling my eyes and moving around him, bumping his shoulder with mine to get some air that isn't full of his woodsy scent. "You're a little late on that front."

"I won't deny it," he agrees. "I can make excuses as to why things happened like they did, but the truth is, I let my career take precedence."

I say nothing.

"I chose success," he continues, turning to face me

41

as I pretend to study the rest of the room. Thankfully, the crew has finished and let us be.

"Shock," I murmur.

"I chose … me."

I stifle a giggle, but it turns into an unattractive snort. Stopping in front of the vanity attached to the dresser, I study my reflection. I look tired, but not overly so. The bags beneath my eyes are only noticeable if you look close enough. My bottom lip is chapped from the amount of times I wet and nibble on it, which I've subconsciously done a lot since watching my book play out in front of me.

My cheeks though … they give me away.

They're colored with the faintest tone of pink, a natural color since Corbin came back into my life. It's hard not to blush when he pays you attention, especially with the memories I have of us together all those years ago.

The touches, kisses, whispers.

We were young and sloppy and invincible back then. That's where we went wrong. Heartbreak was inevitable as soon as we thought nothing could touch us. Eventually, something did.

Reality.

Dreams.

Us.

Looking down, I say, "You always chose yourself, even when you made pretty promises. They were just words and I always knew it. It was my fault for falling for them."

"Kinley—"

"But everything else?" I conclude, meeting his eyes in the mirror. "Everything else was your fault. You can apologize as many times as you want, I forgive you. I forgave you a long time ago because holding onto that resentment was too much."

He's smart enough not to say anything.

"But I'll never forget."

His chin dips in silent acknowledgment.

Taking a deep breath, I paint a smile on my face when I hear people's voices getting nearer. Flattening the wrinkles from my dress, I turn on my heel and watch Corbin play with the candy I shoved at him.

Not knowing what else to say, I walk away and back toward the chair with my name on it. Buchannan is by his, greeting me with a big smile that gives me a weird feeling in my stomach. He stretches out his arms for a hug, which I reluctantly give to him.

He seems nice, but no hug should feel as slimy as his. His hold is too tight and too long and his eyes like to roam where they shouldn't.

Clearing my throat, I say, "The set looks amazing. You guys have brought this to life perfectly."

He touches my arm, and I try not flinching away from the contact. "I'm glad you like it, darling. We should talk more about what you think sometime soon."

I know his intentions aren't innocent, so I simply nod and say nothing as I take my seat. When I look up again, Corbin is glaring at Buchannan with a dark expression on his face.

And for some reason ... I smile.

six

KINLEY / 16

It's dark by the time I clock out and say goodbye to everyone at the restaurant. The Friday night crowd has the bar in the back room packed and the kitchen smelling like onion rings. My stomach growls over the greasy scent as I zip up my jacket and walk out the front doors.

"Hey."

I yelp and swing my arm out of instinct, nearly colliding my fist with the side of Corbin Callum's pretty face.

He dodges the strike by ducking down and raising

45

his hands up in defense. "Whoa! Sorry, I didn't mean to scare you."

My heart is still racing in my chest when I take a step back and stare at him. "Then why are you lurking outside a restaurant at almost ten o'clock at night? That's creepy."

"I saw you inside earlier."

"Still creepy."

He chuckles, shoving his hands in the large pocket of his gray sweatshirt. Instead of the black jeans and tee he sports at school, he's in blue jeans, worn sneakers, and a big hoodie with red AC/DC lettering and the drawstring missing.

His chin dips toward the door. "My family came here to eat dinner and I noticed you were bringing clean glasses out from the back."

I shift my weight from one foot to the other and shiver when a gust of wind smacks into me. "Did you get lost or something? That doesn't explain why you're still here."

His teeth dig into his bottom lip to suppress a smile. "I live across the street. Thought maybe I'd catch up with you when you got done tonight. Say hi."

I blink. "Well ... hi."

I start walking down the gravel driveway that leads to the sidewalk. I'm not sure if I'm really surprised or not that he follows. His footsteps easily match mine until we're walking side by side, coated by the darkness from the blown streetlight.

"Do you need a ride?" he asks, hands still in his pocket.

I shake my head. "I don't live too far."

He continues to follow me. "My mom would kill me if she knew I let you walk home alone in the dark."

"Why?" My nose scrunches. "Is she afraid weird guys are waiting outside restaurants for their unsuspecting victims?"

"Har har."

I grin down at the cracked pavement of the sidewalk the town keeps saying they'll redo.

"It's okay," I assure him, kicking a pebble with the tip of my knock off Converse. "Like I said, I don't live too far from here. Plus, it's mostly lit the whole way."

"Mostly," he repeats. "I've already made it my civic duty to walk with you. Unless you want to walk across the street and let me get my car. I won't even kidnap you."

Rolling my eyes, I glance over at him. "I appreciate that, but it's okay."

"What if I offered you candy?"

"Do you drive a white van too?"

He snorts. "White Jeep, actually."

Now I'm laughing. "My brother once told me I'd get easily kidnapped if someone offered me free pizza. Sad thing is, he's probably not wrong."

"Does that mean you want the ride?"

"Jeeps do have windows…" I shake my head and keep walking, a smile on my face. "But, like I said, I prefer walking."

"Is your brother older or younger?"

"Older."

"Is he your only sibling?"

I nod.

"What's his name?"

"Gavin."

We walk for a few seconds in silence.

Then he breaks it with, "This is the part where you ask me if I have any siblings. The answer is no by the way. I do have a cat named Fred though. He likes to steal the strings from all my hoodies and hoard them under my bed."

My eyes go to his hoodie before I giggle and meet his eyes. "You have a cat named Fred?"

He pulls out his phone and opens his photo gallery before showing me an array of adorable pictures featuring a chubby yellow tiger cat. One of them even shows a pile of strings next to him like they're his most prized possessions.

"He was supposed to be mine," he explains, shrugging. "My mom took a liking to him and they get along better. He just uses me for my hoodies."

I've always wanted a cat. When I was six, I smuggled a stray one into my room using my backpack. It didn't take long for Mom to figure it out because the cat was making weird noises and smelled bad. It was friendly enough with the brightest blue eyes I'd ever seen. Mom fell into a bad allergy attack when she found it and told my Dad to take it to the local shelter.

"We have a dog named Buddy. He's a chocolate lab and one of the sweetest animals. I know he prefers Gavin to me. He sleeps in his bed all the time even though we're not supposed to have animals in them. Mom gave up that fight a long time ago."

We get further down Main Street until some of the other smaller businesses like the art gallery light up the street. People mill about and laugh at something before breaking apart and going their separate ways for the night.

"I've always wanted a cat," I admit, even though at least a minute has passed since the conversation lulled into silence.

"Why haven't you gotten one?"

"My mom is allergic."

He hums out a reply.

Another minute passes before he says, "I guess you could get your cat fix from Fred sometime. He loves the attention."

I slow down, stumbling when my shoe catches on uneven pavement. Corbin grabs my arm to steady me, not letting go until I'm on stable feet again.

"You want me to come to your house?"

"Yeah. Why?"

Nobody invites me to their homes...

"I'd have to ask my parents," I murmur, keeping my gaze locked on the weeds breaking through some of the cracks on the ground.

"Okay." Another pause. "How much further? I'm not trying to get rid of you or anything, but chances are I'll wander in the wrong direction if you don't tell me where to go."

For some reason, that amuses me. "I'm on Alden. Across the street from the cemetery."

"Creepy."

"Not really."

"You ever see Stephen King movies?"

"Don't you mean read Stephen King?"

"That too."

"No to both."

He stops walking. "You've never read or watched anything Stephen King related? *IT*? *Carrie*? *Pet Semetary*?"

When I keep shaking my head, he weaves his hands through his hair until it sticks up in random directions. Clearly he's a King fan, which doesn't surprise me. Gavin read a couple of his books once upon a time and watches almost all his movies.

"That needs to be remedied."

I blink. "It does?"

"Are you scared of horror flicks?"

"I don't know. No?"

"You've never seen a horror movie?"

I shrug.

"What about clowns?"

I'm completely lost. "What about them?"

He cusses under his breath. "We'll start with *Carrie*. It's a classic and not that messed up compared to his other work."

"I didn't agree to watch anything," I remind him, hugging my arms close to my body to warm myself from the cooling wind.

He nods his head toward my street. "Let's go before you freeze to death. You need to watch at least one Stephen King movie before you die."

"Thanks for being a concerned citizen."

His teeth flash with his grin this time.

When we get to my house, he examines the flowerbeds planted in tractor tires on the front lawn, and the decorative windmill between them. Dad made sure everyone who passed the house could see it since the town voted against real windmills being put anywhere in the town limits.

The house is bright red and two stories. There's a tiny basement that offers little standing room, and an attic that nobody has ever been in before. Dad has been renovating the whole thing for years, starting a new project every summer on the outside, and little projects indoors during the wintertime.

"Cute place," he compliments.

"It's home."

He nudges the ground. "How about tomorrow afternoon?"

I stare at him in confusion.

"For the movies?"

"Now we're watching more than one?"

"Is that a yes?"

I sigh heavily. There's no way Dad will let me go to a boy's house to watch movies, especially a stranger. "I have to ask, but I wouldn't get your hopes up. They let my brother do just about anything when he was my age, but that doesn't extend to me."

He playfully pushes my shoulder. "What if I pick you up and put on my charm?"

"I don't think flirting with my dad will help your case any," I deadpan. Then I think about it. "Actually, if he thinks you're gay then you might have a better chance of getting me to come along."

He full on laughs. "Just ask and let me know. I own all King's movies, they're some of my favorites."

"You have others?"

"I'm a movie guy," he states simply.

"Movies can be ... good." I cringe at how lame that comes out, but he doesn't seem to mind.

"Agreed. So, get them to let you come. I'll even have snacks ready. What's your poison? You mentioned pizza. What else?"

He wants to get us pizza? "Uh…"

"It's not a hard question, Little Bird," he muses, sucking in his bottom lip. Even in the dark, his eyes flash a bright color. "What is your favorite food to snack on? Chocolate? Chips? Sour? Swee—"

"Twizzlers," I blurt. "I like Twizzlers."

"Red not black right?"

My nose scrunches at the thought of eating black licorice. Dad loves the stuff. Every time he sees black jellybeans in the store, he gets a bag and snacks on them while watching reruns of crime shows at night.

"Definitely red."

His hand goes to his chest. "A girl after my own heart. We're going to be very good friends, Kinley Thomas."

My lips part, because I never offered that information during our impromptu school tour the other day. "How do you know my name?"

"Simple," he states, backing away. "I asked about you."

Cringing is the best I can do. I can only imagine what people say. He's a senior to my sophomore—two years older. I'm the quiet girl who doesn't offer any answers in class unless I'm forced to talk. At lunch, I tend to sit by myself long enough to eat before going to the gym with a book to read. After school, I go right home instead of participating in any extracurriculars.

I'm not popular.

I don't have many friends.

I'm just … boring.

"Until tomorrow, Little Bird."

"Don't call me that!" I yell after him.

I'm left with his laughter in the night.

THE CONVERSATION I dreaded having with my parents about going to Corbin's house today was anxiety wasted when Corbin showed up at noon and introduced himself to my mother. Dad was out helping Gavin do field work on the farm he's worked on since he graduated, so it made the panic subside. Mom scolded me for not telling her about my plans before asking Corbin about his family's move and what his parents do.

Thankfully, that was all she asked before sending me out the door. If Dad were home, there'd be threats of cleaning shotguns on the front porch while he waited for me to come home. Except we don't own any guns, and our front porch is enclosed, so the fear factor isn't really there like Dad wants.

The short drive to Corbin's house is spent in silence because I don't know what to say. His Jeep smells like the pizza from the gas station down the street, which makes my stomach growl embarrassingly loud. When he parks in the driveway of a pale yellow house, he gets out and grabs a pizza box and a bag full of junk food from the backseat.

I stand beside him, examining the green shrubs lining the sidewalk and the red mailbox next to them. There's a little white fence in the corner where one of the side streets meets Main, and a cute little tree is planted behind it.

"Ready?" Corbin asks, drawing my attention back to him.

"Need help carrying anything?"

He shakes his head and nods toward the door. There are cement steps and black metal railings leading to it, with a brown welcome mat that has little paw print designs all over. I smile as I step over it and into the house, letting Corbin close the door behind us.

The floorplan isn't as open as my house. To my left is staircase that probably leads to all the bedrooms. The hallway in front of us is narrow, but I can see a beige couch and an end table peeking out from around the corner. There's a door on my right that's probably a closet or a bathroom, and I'm sure the kitchen is near the living room. My eyes catch a few different circular patches of wall coloring that looks fresh, and I wonder if they're also renovating.

Corbin heads toward the stairs though. "I could give you a tour if you want, but there's not much to see. I'll show you where the bathroom is up here in case you need to use it, but I have the TV in my room set up and ready for the movies."

"Movie," I correct.

He winks. "If you say so."

I nibble my lip and watch him slowly ascend another step. "Won't your parents think it's rude that I don't introduce myself?"

"They're not home."

My eyes widen. Mom probably thinks someone is here with us or she would have made a fuss. I know Dad wouldn't be happy finding out that I was alone with a boy.

"Kinley?"

I snap out of it, my cheeks blossoming with heat. "Sorry. I just didn't think we were going to be alone."

His lips twitch like he wants to smile, but he refrains. "We can watch the movies in the living room if you want. I'm not planning on doing anything to make you uncomfortable."

I know I'm being stupid. Or overcautious, at the very least. Most girls wouldn't bat an eye at hanging out with Corbin alone in his room. In fact, I'm pretty sure they'd be jealous if they knew I was doing it. I see how most of them watch him and flirt. He's barely been here a month and he's everyone's new favorite thing.

"No, it's fine." I give him a forced smile to back up my words, but I don't know if it looks convincing. I follow him upstairs and glance at the door that Corbin mentions is the bathroom. At the end of a short hall is his room, where a yellow cat is sprawled across his blue comforter.

"This is Fred, right?"

The cat instantly jumps up and rubs against Corbin as he places the pizza and junk food down on the desk next to his bed. I can hear the rumbling purrs from where I stand by the door, smiling as Corbin picks up the cat and brings him over to me.

"Hi, pretty boy." I get a squeaky meow in response, which makes me giggle. Corbin deposits the furry feline in my arms as he grabs the remote and some plates from his desk and sits on the edge of his mattress.

"You can come further in the room, you know. It'll be hard to watch the movie from over there." He gives me an amused smirk as I hesitantly walk over to where he sits and take the seat next to him. Fred climbs off me and nudges Corbin's arm for attention.

Once the movie starts playing, he passes me a plate and then moves Fred to the floor. The cat stretches and watches us as Corbin opens the pizza box and takes out a slice for each of us.

He sits with his back against the wall, biting into his pizza while I stay planted where I am on the edge of the mattress. I pick at the cheese and watch the screen go through its usual copyright warning, trying to distract myself from the boy who is almost definitely staring at me right now.

"Kinley?"

"Hmm?"

"You going to get comfortable?"

"I am."

He snickers and pauses the movie. "Look at me for a sec."

I count to three, then look over my shoulder at his smiling face. His plate of pizza is perched on the leg stretched out straight in front of him, while his other is bent at the knee with his arm resting over it. "I don't bite."

Swallowing, I smile back. "I didn't think you did."

He eyes me. "Why are you sitting there like that then? Hell, you're making *me* uncomfortable."

Staring down at my food, I murmur out a soft apology. I'm not used to this. I've hung out with people before, but usually girls. Unless Gavin had his friends over, which was rare, my time around the opposite sex who isn't related to me is limited.

He pats the spot next to him. "I promise to keep my hands to myself. Can't make that promise about Fred though. He's all paws. I mean, have you seen them? They're disproportional to his body."

From the ground, I hear another meow like he's talking back to Corbin. It makes a genuine smile spread across my face. Taking a deep breath, I slide backwards until my back is pressed against his light blue wall.

I let my eyes go around the room, taking in the shelves lining the opposite wall that have random knick-knacks on them like baseballs, picture frames, books, and movies. Under one of the hanging shelves is a big dresser, with some of the drawers partially open and clothes hanging out—more t-shirts knowing him. The curtains on the only window off to the side are black, and the blinds are down but open so sunlight pours in.

"Are the books by Stephen King?"

"Yep."

"Do you like to read?"

"Just him," he admits.

I nod absentmindedly, studying a picture of him with two older versions of him in one of the black frames on the shelf. They're obviously his parents. I can't tell from here who he gets his eyes from, but his dark hair is from his father. I'm sure at closer inspection I'd get to see where his other features originated too. I'm a clone of my mother, and Gavin is a clone of my father. We both have the same dark brown eye color from Mom though. Dad's eyes are blue, which I always envied. Mom thought it would have been cool to see me get his eye color with her dark brown, almost black, hair—sort of like her father had based on the pictures I'd seen in our old photo albums.

"You good?" he asks, holding up the remote and pressing play again.

I wiggle until I'm settled, my eyes going back to his TV. It's slightly smaller than the one we have at our house, but not by much. "Which one are we starting with?"

"*Carrie.*"

I nod and dig into my pizza.

For the duration of the movie, we're in comfortable silence. I'm surprised by how much I like the movie, considering I've never thought I'd like anything Stephen King related. It's creepy but not too dark, though the electrocution thing was a bit much. Not that some of those kids didn't deserve it.

We eat three-fourths of the pizza before Corbin digs into the junk food. By the end of the movie, we're sharing a pack of red Twizzlers, which we also use as straws for our soda. Gavin taught me how to do it when we were younger, so I showed Corbin our trick which he seemed intrigued with as we downed our Mountain Dew.

When the movie ends, Corbin turns to me with waiting eyes. "Well? What did you think? I know you liked it, but I want you to tell me."

I roll my eyes. "How could you possibly know I liked it?"

He takes another Twizzler. "You'd lean in when it got good, like you couldn't look anywhere else. Did you even notice when Fred came over to get attention from you? Poor guy looked all rejected when you ignored him."

Guilt over my new favorite feline eats at my heart as I search the room for him. "I didn't mean to ignore him. I just wanted to know what happened, especially when they were at the pig pen. Like ... who does that? *Pig's* blood?"

"Do you prefer horse? Sheep? Human?"

My nose scrunches. "Gross."

Corbin moves off the bed and switches the movies before closing the pizza box and gesturing toward the junk food bag in silent inquiry. When I shake my head, he settles back into his spot, resting one ankle over the other.

"I want to do a Stephen King movie," he tells me, shifting his body in my direction.

"Like a play?" There's no way our school would let something like that run. Even if it'd be in higher demand than another rendition of an already famous musical done by thousands of other schools nationwide.

"Like a movie." He rests his head against the wall and studies me. "I want to act. That's what I plan to do with my life. It'd be a dream to be cast for an adaptation of one of his books. Even a remake of a film already out."

"Like *Carrie*?"

He shrugs. "Why not? He's the only author I read, and I've seen all his movies. It'd be a huge achievement to be part of it as a professional."

"Acting," I repeat quietly. "Cool."

"What about you?"

"I don't act."

"What do you want to do?"

The answer is on the tip of my tongue, but I'm embarrassed to admit it. It isn't like I aspire to be a rodeo clown or something, but everyone who knows what I enjoy doing in my pastime doesn't understand it. They think it's a hobby rather than a legitimate career path.

He pokes my nose, making me go cross-eyed to look at his finger. "I see the wheels turning in your head. What is it?"

I sigh, knowing I have nothing to lose. "I want to be a professional writer—an author. I've written ever since I could hold a pencil, and the more I get asked about what I want to do in the future, the more I realize how much I want to get my books published."

Part of me expects him to give me a funny look, like he's wondering why I'd ever want something so random. People in small towns are raised to think practically. Being an author isn't like being a farmer, or nurse, or teacher. That's what people around here become. Except, I don't want that.

"I think that's awesome," he states, giving me a smile that's anything but cocky or mischievous like normal.

I blink. "You do?"

Nodding, he says, "I don't see why it wouldn't be. Seems like the perfect job for you. You like books and writing, so the whole author thing makes sense."

"Most people don't see it that way."

"Most people aren't us."

Us?

Seeing the confusion on my face, he decides to elaborate. "Few people ever act on their dreams, especially in places like this. It takes special kind of people to live them out. I'm going to act no matter what it takes. I'm willing to make sacrifices even if people don't approve. You seem like you'd do the same to get a book published."

I would.

Something in my chest lightens. Nobody has ever understood before. It feels nice to be in the same mindset as someone instead of pretending like it's okay that they don't get my dreams.

He hits play on the next movie. "We're going to be bigger than this town, Little Bird. Just you wait and see."

I'm not sure I want to be bigger than this town. I'm not sure I don't either.

seven

CORBIN / Present

THE BEDROOM on set has a four-poster king sized bed directly in the middle of it. The soft white bedding is eerily familiar, like I've seen it somewhere before. On either side are light wooden nightstands—one with a lamp, the other with a book and alarm clock. Surrounding the furniture are cameras and lights to create the perfect shadowing and highlights for at least three different angles.

It's our first sex scene today, and I notice Kinley lingering outside of set staring at the placement of everything like she's lost in thought. One of her hands holds the wall, her entire right side leaning against it keeping her up.

Nobody bothers her as she takes it all in, and I wonder what's going through her mind. Is she still mad about the picture? Is she cursing me? It's probable.

I've read the script twice. This scene is pivotal in cementing Ryker and Beck's forbidden relationship. Every moral is questioned and played out in sultry, sexy detail through caresses, touches, and pleas.

That's when it hits me—the bedding, the books on the nightstand, everything. I cuss, letting out a strangled, *"fuck me"* loud enough to get Kinley's attention while I stare at her.

This is like a grander version of her bedroom growing up. From the white down blanket with five pillows lining the top of the bed to the folded gray throw at the end. The book on the stand isn't the Stephen King novel she'd sometimes read to me when I procrastinated from homework or practicing lines. Honestly, I'd just wanted to hear her voice.

Kinley blinks. A light pink color settles into her cheeks again as she breaks contact and stares at the floor. She knows I've made the connection.

But why?

Olivia walks up beside me. "We should see how she wants us to do this. You know, ask if there's a specific way she wants our characters to act. I'm sure she has a vision."

I snort at that, causing Liv to give me a weird look. Brushing it off, I follow her over to where Kinley stands.

"Hey," Liv greets, smiling at Kinley. "Callum and I were wondering if you had any notes for us. Should our characters touch a certain way? Hesitate? Go all in?"

Nobody else knows that the slightest widening of Kinley's eyes means she's internally freaking out. She hates not being prepared for a question because she freezes.

"Uh..." She chokes out a nervous laugh, only watching Olivia. "I didn't really think about it. I'm sure whatever is in the script for it will be fine. I trust you."

She didn't emphasize that she trusted both of us, which I file away under things to let get under my skin at a later date. Preferably not one when I'll be filmed practically naked rolling around a bed with my co-star while my ex watches from the sidelines. I know damn well where she got some of the inspiration for this setup, but I wouldn't call her out.

Olivia thinks she's helping when she asks, "What about channeling from a past experience? I'm sure you wanted the scene between Beck and Ryker to be a certain way. When I read the book, it gave me chills. Their chemistry is undeniable. They're soulmates, even when they shouldn't be."

Kinley's lips part. "You've read the book?"

Olivia perks up. "I'm a big fan of your work to be

WHERE THE LITTLE BIRDS GO

honest. When I heard they were picking up rights to the film, I made my agent keep tabs on casting calls. You have no idea how happy I am to be Beck."

All Kinley does is blink.

"So," Liv presses, "should we try recreating the book the best we can? They did a pretty good job adapting it for the script, don't you think?"

A nod.

"There's almost a nervousness to Beck," Olivia continues, practically bouncing where she stands. "I love that about her. She's normally confident, but her love for Ryker makes her vulnerable. It was one of my favorite parts."

I'm having trouble swallowing.

"Was it based on anything real?"

I'm choking on my own spit but manage to keep my cool while my eyes pierce Kinley's. She still refuses to make eye contact with me, so I cross my arms on my chest and watch her squirm. Call me a dick, but I'm enjoying it.

"Not ... well, no. Not really."

My eyes narrow.

"Do writers ever draw from experiences?"

If I wasn't so pissed at Kinley's blatant lying, I'd be amused over Liv. She's practically fangirling her. Shit, I didn't even know she'd read the book. I bet she's read all of Kinley's titles two times over and I know there's a lot of them. Between Mom updating

67

me and keeping tabs on local Lincoln news when another one makes a bestseller list I get my fill of everything Kinley Thomas. It's an unhealthy obsession.

Liv fires off more questions. "Are there any experiences worth writing about? Like, there's an innocence to this scene, you know? Even though Beck and Ryker are far from virgins, they treat every moment with each other like it's their first. To think you might have had that ... ugh. I'm jealous just thinking about it. Your first time must have been amazing."

Without blinking, Kinley says, "Or so bad that I've had to compensate through fictional sex over the years."

My jaw drops.

Olivia bursts out laughing until there are actual tears in her eyes. "Oh my God. I didn't even think of that. You're officially my hero. Was it really that bad? Did he finish in like two seconds? That's what happened to me. It might have been like ten seconds, but I was kind of relieved because of how bad it hurt."

That gets my attention.

Kinley's face is bright red. "I don't really think about it. It's in the past."

Olivia giggles. "You're too nice. I bet you're just trying to save the guy's dignity. Let me guess. He didn't even ask if you were okay. Most guys think it's as good for us as it is them."

My nostrils flare. "Give the guy a break. Do girls

tell guys what it's like their first time? Get vocal about what it's like? No."

Two sets of eyes land on me.

It's Liv who says, "You don't have to defend some guy you don't even know just because you share the same German sausage, Callum. You don't understand the crap women get put through just to try getting a guy who knows what a clit is and how to work it."

"And girls aren't honest about if it hurts or if they like something." My eyebrow quirks and I try not looking at Kinley but fail. "I'm just saying, not all men are total assholes in the bedroom."

Olivia shoves my shoulder. "Take many virgins to bed, huh? Listen, don't get your panties in a twist. We're just pointing out that men have it better than women when it comes to sex."

Kinley clears her throat. "I don't really have notes for you guys about the scene. If you read the book, you know there's something unspoken between Ryker and Beck. Like everything between them is wrong but..."

"Effortless," I finish quietly.

Kinley whispers, "Yeah."

Olivia nudges me. "If that's your way of saying you read the book, then maybe I have some hope for your species about how to give a girl an orgasm."

She pats my shoulder before shooting Kinley a wink and walking off to whoever is calling her name.

"Kinley—"

She steps back. "Please don't." Her voice is barely audible, which makes my jaw tick. "Not here. Not now."

Buchannan chooses then to give us a five-minute warning to take our places. I see Kinley visibly ease, and hear the softest breath escape her flushed lips. She's relieved.

Unfortunately for her, I'm not letting it go that easily. "Beck admits to Ryker that she wishes she could go back and change everything. You trying to tell me that you don't find some truth in that, Little Bird?"

Her nose twitches. "I'm not her."

I back up, hands raising. "Aren't you?"

KINLEY IS GETTING ready to leave when I jog over to the car she's heading for and stop the backdoor from opening. It shouldn't surprise me that she opted not to wait for me while I finished the final scene of the day. She's avoided me at all costs, disappeared during the lunchbreak, and barely made eye contact with me for more than two seconds.

The only time she paid me any attention was when Olivia or Buchannan was around to get her feedback on what she'd seen during the day. I could tell Liv wanted her approval of the sex scene, which Kinley undoubtedly gave us. It was the way she looked at us after Buchannan called cut that made me realize we nailed it exactly how she wanted—the softest glaze of tears, the slightest lip part. She loved it, even if she didn't want to.

"We need to talk," I say, keeping my palm against the side of the car so she's not tempted to try diving into the back.

"No, we don't."

Sighing, I reach behind me and pull the package of Twizzlers out from my pocket that she gave back to me this morning. Holding them out to her, I watch as she stares unblinkingly at the candy.

I shake it. "They're not poisoned. I can't guarantee they're not stale though since they stayed open all day. Plus, I got them from the vending machine, so who knows when the expiration is even good on them."

Slowly, her fingers wrap around them as she draws them to her side. "You got me candy from a vending machine?"

"Would have gotten them from a store, but I didn't have a lot of time between takes. Had someone bring them over to the hotel to deliver with dinner since you left early that day," I answer easily, giving her a small smile.

She wets her lips. "Thanks."

I tap the car. "So … talk?"

"We are talking."

I all but growl. "You know damn well this isn't the kind of conversation I've been waiting to have all day.

In case you've forgotten, you gave my ego a little beat down earlier."

"I didn't—"

"Did you write about us?"

She blinks.

I blink back.

After a moment of awkward silence, she shifts her weight and sighs. "I didn't write this about you. You've probably read the whole script, right? This story isn't our story. We don't have one."

"Everyone has a story," I argue.

"That's not what I mean," she mutters, her shoulders tensing. "Our past isn't the kind of story I want publicized. I'll always have pieces of personal experience in every book, but that doesn't mean any of us finds its way onto a page."

My mind backtracks to the bed. "What about the set decorations?"

No answer.

Not willing to give up, I ask, "If I searched in the wicker bins off to the side of that set, would I find a stash of candy? Comic books? Movies? I don't think it's a coincidence that the scene we shot this morning was in a room identical to the one that we made a lot of memories in."

"Corbin—" Her voice cracks. "Stop."

"Why?" I throw my hands up. "Just tell me, Kinley! Is it really so hard to admit that you wrote your bedroom into that book? That you channeled something about us into those characters? I heard what Olivia said."

Her eyes stare holes into the pavement under her strappy heeled sandals. Bright blue nail polish peeks out from the ends, which makes me shake my head. She always insisted on wearing neon colors. Blue was her favorite, but it couldn't be any other shade than the one currently greeting my gaze.

"You don't understand how much it hurts," she finally tells me, meeting my eyes with a distance in hers that caves my chest. "I don't want to think about the past. There's a lot I'm proud of and wouldn't change, but there's also stuff that hurts too much to think about for long. You can probably guess which is which."

My jaw ticks. "We both had dreams, Kinley. You told me you'd support me no matter what it took."

"I meant it."

"So why do you hate me?"

"I don't—"

I hit the car with my closed fist, leaving the tiniest dent in the top. Kinley steps back and stares at the blemish, before her eyes ever so slowly meet mine again.

Taking a deep breath, I shove both hands into my pockets that way she won't see them shaking. "Don't lie to me. I'm not going to pretend like I didn't know you were upset with my decision to leave back then, but I thought you understood how much I wanted this life."

Her jaw tightens. "And I thought you knew how much I expected you to come back like you promised. Remember? You said 'I'm coming back for you, Kinley. Trust me.' I was stupid enough to believe it, Corbin. Do you know how pathetic I looked waiting for a phone call? A text? An email? *Anything*?

"My mom kept telling me to try distracting myself because I'd waste all my time focusing on when you were going to reach out or show up. Weeks went by. Months. After a while, I finally listened to her. I channeled everything I had into my books, choosing to build a fictional world where nobody could hurt me like you did. I was in control for the first time. I got to decide what happened instead of being suspended in time until some teenage guy that my brother warned me away from made good on his promise."

My hands go to my hair, weaving through the gelled-up strands that hair and makeup put in earlier for the last scene. I know a losing battle when I see it, and Kinley is about to sink the last battleship I have. Opening my mouth would make me sink faster, and I'm not ready to drown.

"Thinking about you, *seeing you*, causes me the worst kind of pain," she finishes, grabbing ahold of the door handle. "I tried getting my agent to make them cast someone else, just to let you know. Or to pull the project. My agent told me I was being stupid. *'Corbin Callum will make this movie a box office success.'* I had to put aside my pride for you again when my pride should have always come first."

I close my eyes and palm them with the heels of my hands. "Kinley … shit."

"You…" Her voice breaks. "I hate how much you bring Ryker to life, but you do. You're perfect for him. That's probably the worst part of this whole experience."

My hands fall to my sides. "Seeing me as the leading role?"

She shakes her head. "Having to share this dream with you when I swore to myself that you'd be nothing but a distant memory for good."

Fuck that hurt. *Bad.* But knowing I deserve nothing less, I stand back while she opens the car door and closes it behind her. The glass isn't as tinted as my car, so I can see her stare at me with eyes void of emotion. They're nothing but empty brown pits, with my reflection in the middle falling into an endless abyss.

When the car pulls away, I find myself standing in the middle of the lot looking like the biggest dumbass on the planet because I let her go. *Again.*

But did I really have a choice this time?

She doesn't know what her brother told me shortly after I came back to visit my family. He painted a vivid picture of what he'd do if I reached out to her before she was ready, but I thought he was messing around. Until his fist met my jaw and nearly broke the fucking thing. When my mother confirmed that Kinley was the shell of a girl I'd introduced her to the first time, I knew I fucked up.

I'd been determined to make something of myself so the harm I caused would be worth it—so I could show something for it. The harder I worked, the further I became from making good on anything I'd told people when I left. I remember when people joked about never forgetting where I come from.

But I did.

Because the fame has always been my focus, not the town who patted me on the back like they doubted I could make something of myself. I fed my determination until I'd become successful, and by then I had little control over the promises I'd spoken.

I told myself this was all for Kinley.

But I'm selfish son of a bitch.

A liar.

This has always been for me.

eight

KINLEY / Present

THE SECOND NOTE shows up a few days later, slipped under my door sometime during the night. I went to bed after giving up on my writing deadline, too distracted by the events of the week.

When I saw the envelope resting on the carpet, I debated on leaving it there or kicking it under the rug so I wouldn't be tempted to open it. I'm not that strong though, and that's probably the hardest part to admit.

Maybe we're more addicted to the pain than to each other.
-Ryker

STARING at the words for a fourth time, I sigh and set the note down by the empty candy wrapper. Around eleven last night I decided to eat my feelings in the form of red licorice. At some point, my sugared-up brain decided it was a good idea to Google Corbin Callum and torture myself with articles and interviews of the man who's a complete stranger to me now.

The two hours I spent watching YouTube videos of red-carpet interviews made me remember the few times we joked in the past about making it to black tie events. He never had a doubt that he'd walk the carpet, but me? We were always different in that way. Corbin had a natural confidence to him that I always secretly envied. He carried himself without a care in the world while I let all mine rest on my shoulders so openly for the world to see.

Video clip after video clip, I would study how well he pulled off a tuxedo like I hadn't seen him in one at winter formal. His body is nothing like it was though. He's filled out in all the right places, ripples of muscle he's clearly worked hard on showcased over every inch of him. Even his face—his cut jaw and narrow cheeks—

has a new shape that only age and exercise could give him after all this time.

The first time I saw him on set, I considered cutting out sugar because I know under my clothes is a softness that jiggles when I move a certain way. Despite the time spent doing at-home workouts every day, my thick thighs remain. Maybe if I didn't turn to carbs and sugar in times of stress, I'd finally squeeze into a size four again instead of jumping into a seven.

Blowing out a breath, I move away from the written-on stationary that I folded into a tiny origami bird and get dressed. Buchannan mentioned doing reshoots this morning with some of the smaller roles, so I'm not going in until this afternoon. It gives me time to tour around the city and get away from the world I stepped willingly back into.

As I pass the folded note again, I grab the waste basket and brush everything from the table into it, leaving it by the door in hopes someone will empty it before I'm back. I don't want to see the handwriting in the paper animal I've loved making since he made up that stupid nickname for me.

All I see when I glance down is Ryker's name staring back at me, and I wonder why I let myself get to this point. We can't keep playing this game because there's too much to lose. His name brings the press, and mine brings the backlash. One wrong move, and not only his fans will come after me, but his wife's fans too.

But I think about his departing words the other day despite trying to bury them.

I've always been Beck.

He's always been Ryker.

And we're masochists—addicted to the pain.

nine

KINLEY / 16

BLACK INK SMUDGES across the side of my palm, leaving traces of unreadable letters on the notebook paper in front of me. Frowning, I wipe my hand on my blue jeans and try making out what I wrote just seconds prior. My mind has been scrambled with a few different story ideas that have distracted me from taking proper notes in class. I'm not even sure what we went over in Geometry today.

Just as I'm about to flip the page and continue where I left off, the subtle scent of fresh soap and French vanilla coffee hits my nose as a chair is pulled back. My lips curve upward when Corbin plants himself next to me, eyeing the notebook.

"Writing again?"

"Yep."

He eyes the ink stain on my pants. "You know there's this thing called soap and water. I hear it works wonders when people's hands are dirty."

Rolling my eyes, I click my pen against the table and lean back. "I doubt you came here to tell me about proper hygiene."

"It's lunch."

I blink.

He sighs and pulls something from his backpack, which rests next to him on the table. I smile when I see the familiar red licorice package resting like a center-piece between us.

He watches me peel open the plastic and pull one of the Twizzlers out. "You should eat something that has more dietary nutrition than sugar, but at least you won't starve the rest of the day. Then I'll have to hear about how hungry you are on the way home, and you'll guilt me into buying you something at the gas station with even worse nutritional value."

I grin. "I'm not planning on being a famous actor, which means I can consume all the sugar I want."

He huffs, making me grin wider. "I'll remind you of that when you're sobbing on the phone to me because you can't fit into your formal dress."

"Why would I need a formal dress?"

"When you come to the Oscars with me," he dead-pans, as if to say *duh*. "I suppose it could also be for whatever author awards are identical to the Oscars."

"The RITA Awards."

He stares at me.

I bite down onto my licorice. "It's the highest award a romance writer can get for the genre. It's an award given by the Romance Writers of America group."

"Huh." His brows furrow. "Sounds like it's a big deal then."

"Is an Oscar a big deal?"

"Uh ... yeah."

I just stare until he gets my point.

He steals some of the candy. "Anyway, when we're both famous we should go to events together. You can go to the Oscars with me and I'll go to the RITA Awards with you."

I study him, wondering if he means that. Corbin has been here for about two months. In that time frame, he's made plenty of other friends. Mostly guys, but some girls who make it obvious they want to be more. I've seen him flirt with some of them, which makes me roll my eyes every time. He teases me about being jealous when I pick on him for the thorough eye groping he gets from Shelly Fisher, so in retaliation I gave Shelly his number and said he wanted her to have it. He didn't find that as amusing as I did.

"What if I can't fit into my dress?"

He shrugs casually. "I'll have enough money to hire someone to tailor it.

My eyes narrow. "What if one of us is dating someone else?"

He snorts in an unattractive way, making me giggle. "When will we have time to date? We're barely going to have time for ourselves."

I lower my candy. "You honestly think you'll remain single? Don't be stupid, Corbin. Nobody who amounts to anything in the acting world is ever single for long."

When he doesn't try to argue, I nod.

I can understand his determination not to get distracted by other people. It's the same mindset I have. The writing world is competitive, which means your book needs to be unique in order to get a lot of attention. As a writer, you have to stand out against the rest of the crowd. If that means becoming the crazy cat lady until I make something of myself, then so be it.

"What are you writing?" Corbin asks, instead of continuing our last conversation.

My arm covers the jumbled words. "I found a website for aspiring writers online. They host contests that have pretty cool prizes."

"Like?"

"Chances to get published."

His brows shoot up. "So, you're writing a story for one of the competitions?"

I nod, glancing at the words that don't quite make sense yet.

He smiles, which makes his expression softer. I prefer it to the look he gives girls in the halls, where he winks and smirks and makes most of the female (and some male) student population swoon. I usually laugh at how easy it is for them to fall under his spell, but it gets annoying too.

"You'll win, Little Bird."

Not bothering to correct him on the name that he insists on calling me, I ask, "How do you know? The story could be horrible."

He drapes his arm on the back of the chair he's tipping back in. "Nothing you could do is horrible. Plus, you submitted a story for the English department newsletter last year, which Mrs. Bishop has in her classroom."

My cheeks heat. "You read that?"

"It's good, Kinley."

Kinley, not Little Bird. "Thanks. I'm hoping to win at least one of these contests. The other prizes are talking to published authors one on one and asking them questions to understand their process."

"Anyone I know?"

"Nicholas Sparks."

He pauses. "*The Notebook* guy?"

"That's one of his," I confirm, tapping my pen against the paper. "Anyway, it'd be cool to know what they do to focus on their books. Some of my favorite authors have families and other responsibilities. I want to know how they balance everything."

He hums and reaches for the notebook, but I slap his hand away. Holding it to his chest like a big baby, he frowns. "You could have hurt me, Little Bird. Is there a deadline that's making you violent? Perhaps protein deficiency from lack of proper food?"

I keep the notebook out of his reach. "I don't like people reading my stuff when it's not at its best, especially people I know."

"Why?"

"Would you want people seeing you act when your craft isn't perfected?"

He shakes his head.

"Then you understand."

He sighs and scrapes the chair back. "Just eat your Twizzlers so you don't whine to me later about skipping out on lunch."

I make a face at him. "The only decent thing they have is peanut butter and jelly. I'll be there tomorrow. Save me a seat amidst your biggest fans."

He chuckles as he walks away. "Still sound jealous, Little Bird."

"Think again!"

The librarian shushes me with a single glance, causing me to sink down into my chair. When Corbin is long gone, I stare at my words and nibble my bottom lip. When my pen meets the paper, the story flows right out of me.

A MONTH LATER, I'm scrambling out the door in a rush with Mom yelling after me about a jacket and a piece of paper dangling from my hand. I usually never run unless something with sharp teeth is chasing me, but today is the exception. My sneakered feet take me all the way down Alden and onto Main, where people stare at me as I weave through the Saturday Folk Festival crowd that gathers around the bank parking lot for hippie music and fruit pie.

When I see the yellow house from a distance, my grip on the now wrinkled paper tightens and a smile plasters on my face. I'd normally be nervous over what his parents thought about me showing up out of the blue, but I met them both a few weeks ago when Corbin asked me to come over and watch more movies. Not Stephen King, but a comedy he'd gotten to break up the horror fest. His dad had greeted me first, and it was obvious that Corbin was Mr. Callum's clone right from his silver eyes and prominent straight nose, to the quirk of his lips that screamed charm. His mother was gorgeous, and her warm personality reminded me a lot of my new friend when he encouraged me to write. He was a perfect mixture of the two.

As I run up the sidewalk that leads to the walkway,

I begin slowing my steps enough to catch my breath. Mrs. Callum is in the front yard raking orange and yellow leaves with her husband a few feet away. When they hear the crunch of the late fall foliage under my feet, they both turn and smile at me.

"Morning, Kinley," Mrs. Callum says first, her eyes bright as she rests the rake against her side. "Corbin is inside with a couple of friends. You can go in."

My lips part as I suck in some much-needed oxygen into my tight lungs. "I didn't know he had company." I glance at the paper and then back at them. "I can just show him another—"

Mr. Callum walks over to me. "Don't be silly. Come in. I was just about to put on some hot water for tea. Do you want any? We also have hot chocolate."

Corbin's father makes me wonder if he'll sound the same when he's older—gravelly and sweet, but also blunt and demanding. It wouldn't hurt if Corbin also aged like him too, but I keep that little tidbit to myself.

Corbin never mentioned hanging out with anyone today when we talked last night, so I'm not sure if agreeing to go inside is a good idea. The cold air against my body is making my hands shake, and I know Mom will give my blue skin one good look before saying *I told you so* when I get back.

"I wouldn't mind cocoa," I admit, following him inside. He holds the door open for me like Corbin does every time I'm over, before closing it and leading me into the kitchen.

From upstairs, I hear laughter. The louder tone is undoubtedly Corbin and makes me smile. The others I don't know though. One of them even sounds pitchy, girly, and I feel like maybe I should make up an excuse to go home and leave him to whatever is going on.

"I forgot," I blurt, jabbing my hand toward the door. "I just remembered that I promised my mom I'd help her clean the house today."

Internally cringing at the poor excuse, I turn toward the door and shoot Mr. Callum a quick wave before walking out. The laughter dies down as I pass the stairs, and I hear Mr. Callum call my name which causes me to walk a lot faster before anyone else can hear him.

I'm fighting the wind that's picking up my loose hair with its brutal gusts when I hear a different voice call out after me. I stop in the middle of the sidewalk just as Corbin jogs over to where I'm standing.

"Hey." His smile is no different than usual, which makes me feel a little better. The last thing I want is to bother him when he's with his other friends. I even like some of them, like Zach Russo. He's two years older than me like Corbin is, and not nearly as annoying as the boys in my sophomore class. He'll even say hi to me in the hallway, and not just when Corbin is around.

"I didn't know you had people over." I lick my lips and gesture toward the house. "Sorry about just showing up. I should have texted you or something to see if—"

He nudges my shoulder. "Don't worry about it, Kinley. What's up?" His eyes look down at the paper in my hand. "What is that?"

The smile on my face reappears. "It's what I wanted to show you. I got so excited that I bolted out my house like it was on fire."

He laughs and reaches down, taking the paper and studying what's written on it. When he glances up at me, the prideful smile showcased on his face makes my fingertips tingle.

"You won."

I nod enthusiastically. "They chose the winner last night, but I didn't see the email until this morning. As soon as I saw it I squealed. Mom thought I found another mouse in my room which freaked her out. She hates mice."

"Noted."

"Anyway," I press on, jumping. "I won a chance to talk to a bestselling author and get my story published in a literary magazine!"

He draws me in for a hug and squeezes me to his body. Melting into his warmth, I wrap my arms around his midsection, burying my nose into his chest. We've never done this before, but I like it.

I pull away first when he asks, "Who's the author you get to talk to?"

"I have no idea."

His laugh bursts out of him. When I meet his amused gaze, I can't help but laugh too. In the bright November sunlight, a rarity between cold snaps and snow flurries, I notice the prominent scar on his eyebrow. We exchanged war stories about our scars not long ago. He was chasing Fred around the house when he lost his footing and slammed his head into the corner of the coffee table, leaving the slightest white scar across his brow. I remember how embarrassed he was to admit that he'd been wounded because of his cat.

"But," I amend, pulling my focus back to the contest, "it doesn't matter. Do you want to know why? I may not have heard of them, but *someone* has. And in turn, they'll have heard about me. Even if they forget about my existence after we're done talking."

"Nobody could forget you, Little Bird."

I scoff. "Stop. Did you forget the bestselling part? They're busy being successful. The last thing they're going to think about in their free time is the girl from a town they've never heard of in the middle of nowhere."

"It's still your name out there."

Grinning, I take the paper back. "True."

"I'm proud of you. Seriously."

For the first time since I arrived at his place, I take a deep breath. "I'm proud of me too. It may not be much, but it's something. Anyway, I'll let you get back to your friends. I need to go put on like forty layers to warm up."

He notes my lack of outerwear. "It's like forty today. Where is your jacket?"

I roll my eyes. "At home, *Mom.*" Sticking my tongue out as I back up, I hug the paper to my chest. He mimics me, making me laugh.

"For the record, you're my friend too."

I wave it off. "Whatever. I bet you're making them watch Stephen King movies and droning on for hours about everything King does in his free time."

He winks. "But I don't feed them while doing it. Especially not our favorite candy. You should feel special, Little Bird."

The annoying part is, I do.

ten

CORBIN / Present

THE DIM LIGHT from the floor lamp by the leather sectional I'm sitting on is the only thing letting me skim through the script to prepare for tomorrow. My obsession with picking apart every sentence is consuming me, yet I can't force myself to go to bed until I've combed through the lines I'm supposed to deliver like the person who created them isn't assessing the entire delivery.

My palm scrapes down my tired face as I pick up my phone and glance at the time. I'm usually going through useless emails that my agent sends me thinking I'll pay attention to them by now, or already in bed.

Half the shit littering my inbox and messages are different opportunities for sponsorships and commercials that would line my pockets until my next big job.

The team who represents me also knows that I ignore most of what they send me because I don't want my name tied to a product or think it's a complete waste to begin with. There have only been a few times in my past where I settled on doing a quick job for cash when I needed it, but I'm not the young kid starting out anymore.

Dropping my phone on my couch when I see a voicemail from Mom, I lean back and groan loudly into the room. We speak once or twice a month because my schedule is busy. Ever since I signed onto the *Through Shattered Glass* movie, she's been asking for updates on how things have been going.

By things, she means Kinley.

My mother's enthusiasm over Kinley's movie gets me hounded with questions about how her *favorite girl* is doing because she hasn't seen her in so long. Mom always wanted a daughter and treated Kinley like her own. It made having Kinley around easier because the mistakes I made stopped becoming the focus of all our conversations—especially with Dad.

The thought of *Mr. Callum* sours my mood instantly, causing me to peel myself from the couch and head into my bedroom to change. I would try over and over again to impress my parents only to be criticized and doubted by the man I'm so much alike. Kinley always understood where I came from because her family struggled getting why she went after writing like she needed it to breathe.

Her and I are alike in all the ways that matter, which made us inseparable. Having her in my life made everything easier. My family got along better, we got to root each other on when it came to writing contests and auditions, and when things didn't work out we were there for one another to vent to.

Slipping into my nylon running shorts, my eyes catch the two little black lines on my left pec. Staring at them in the mirror, I run the pad of my thumb over the ink. Everyone asks about them, but they remain a mystery. Makeup usually covers the simple tattoos for movies, but Buchannan let me keep them visible during my shirtless scenes. It seems symbolic given the history and the woman who started it all.

Two lines. Two strikes. They represent the moments I realized that I loved Kinley Thomas—loved her as a friend and more. Far more. Press always wants the inside scoop on why I bothered with something so plain, so permanent. Most actors stray from marks like this. But I wanted a reminder of the feelings that stuck with me for so long. She's always been a part of me and always will be.

Covering my chiseled torso with a loose sleeveless tee, I head into my spare room that's been converted into a makeshift gym. The equipment isn't as impressive as some of the professional places I've been to with my trainer, but it gets the job done when I work myself up and need to release my anger.

Right now, I'm full of it.

Because I can't change how anyone sees me—the press, my peers, my family. It's easier to ignore the opinions of people when they're not related to you, but a different story when your own father is focused on the negative rather than something good. I can't be the household name the same way Kinley is in Lincoln because the press made me out to be the playboy. The partier. The guy nobody can take seriously.

I was pictured at a party with two former co-stars who were known for substance abuse, so everyone assumed I was into drugs too. Some other asshole at a party a few weeks after that got a video of me smoking a joint with a few people that only sparked the rumors over me upgrading to something heavier. I'll never forget being asked by my parents if I'm clean, like they expect me to admit I'm not. My father's distant tone on the phone that day had cemented how I felt about him despite my denial that I'm doing drugs. Our relationship, which was always strained, became nonexistent.

I run faster on the treadmill until I struggle breathing. The images that swirl in the back of my mind range from some of the best and worst moments I've had since the day I told Kinley I'd be back. No longer is my

WHERE THE LITTLE BIRDS GO

resentment trained on my father, but of the girl who I still want.

Nearly tripping when my shoe catches the other, I pull the safety pin and climb off the machine. Hunched over with my palms resting above my slightly bent knees, I curse at myself as I try catching my breath.

I wonder if this is what it feels like for her when she sees me on set. *Thinking about you, seeing you, causes me the worst kind of pain.* Is the pain like a burn to the lungs every time she sees me going over set notes? Laughing with my co-stars? Living my dream? All I know is that it fucking hurts to think of her too.

Of the times we watched movies.

Of the times we went out on long drives.

We shared a lot—secrets about our families, things nobody else knew because we were afraid how we felt made us bad people. I know the innerworkings of Kinley like nobody else does.

Did. I *did* know her.

Straightening, I punch the wall as hard as I can as I pass by it. The hole left behind is nothing compared to the anger simmering in my stomach over something I can't change.

She didn't want me casted.

She wanted them to pull the fucking plug.

She doesn't understand that I demanded the role as soon as I realized her name was tied to the movie. I shouldn't have. It makes me scum to need her in my life in any form I can get it like I have a right to claim her time. But I did, and here we are a year after the decisions were made over who would make this an Oscar-worthy performance.

A second hole is left in the hallway.

eleven

KINLEY / Present

TEARS BLUR my vision as I watch Olivia's hands shake as they wrap around her phone. Her body slumps forward as her breathing hitches, the camera moving closer to capture the name on the phone as her fingers let it drop.

"I'm sorry," she whimpers, fingers going to her hair. The cell remains screen-up on the floor, her fiancé's picture staring back at her as she opens her eyes.

Corbin comes into the shot, kneeling beside where Olivia sits on the couch. When he reaches out, she jerks back and shakes her head.

"Beck," he says, voice breaking as she abruptly stands up and backs away from him.

Her hands wipe at her cheeks desperately, her skin red and her hair a mess. "I can't keep doing this, Ryker. Don't you see that? It's not fair to him."

Corbin stands. "What about us?"

Olivia keeps shaking her head.

Corbin steps forward, leaving plenty of distance between them. "What about how unfair we're being to this opportunity? You can't just say you're sorry and leave it at that."

Hands cupping her face, Olivia tries evening her breathing before looking at Corbin again. "This was a mistake. It's always a mistake with you, Ryker. We're trapped and we're bringing everyone down with us."

This time Corbin moves right in front of her, tipping her chin up. "We'll keep making the same mistakes because we never want to learn."

Olivia pushes his hand away. "Then we're masochists."

Corbin smiles at her in a way that is far too familiar. It's the same smirk he shot girls in the hallway at school. The very same one he'd give me when he was up to no good.

"Welcome to love, baby."

I blink when Buchannan calls cut and lean back in my chair. Not realizing I'd been sitting forward as they acted out the scene, I quickly wipe away a stray tear and smile when Olivia looks at me.

Both she and Corbin walk over to where I sit, but it's Olivia who embraces me in a tight hug. "I can't believe you're crying." Stepping back, she swipes her own cheeks. "That scene made me tear up the first time I read it. It's like Beck can't decide who she's sorrier to —Ian or Ryker."

Swallowing, I take a deep breath. "I think when I wrote it I wanted her to feel guilt for what she's putting them both through. But..." My eyes sneak a peek at Corbin before going back to Olivia's waiting gaze. "I think she feels sorry for herself because she knows she deserves more but can't allow herself happiness without misery."

"Hence the masochist thing," Olivia concludes in understanding. "It'd be amazing to live in that head of yours for a day. Is that really how you view love? Painfully?"

Pausing, I contemplate giving an honest answer. I've thought about love a lot of times, so I know what I believe. As a romance writer, it's important to have a different view when you're selling the chemistry written on paper.

"I think real love is almost impossible to find without some form of pain along the way," I answer truthfully, feeling emotion swell in the back of my throat. "Sometimes you find it with the wrong person at the wrong time and sometimes…" I force a tight smile. "Sometimes you find it with the right person at the wrong time and realize you can't keep it. Either way, there's pain that comes with opening yourself up to somebody."

Olivia reaches out and takes my hand, squeezing it once. "That's why I love your books. You don't write about false hope like love is some easy to acquire thing. It hurts."

I simply nod at her in agreement.

She let's go of my hand and adds, "But I think that the right person will come along again when the time is right. You know, if it's meant to be and all that bullshit."

Choking out a laugh, I glance at Corbin. His eyes are burning into mine, causing me to look back at Olivia and pretend like the source of my belief isn't witnessing my emotional turmoil.

"You guys did amazing," is all I say in return, smiling at them both to get my point across. Gripping the arms of the chair, I scope out the crew moving on to the next set they're shooting on. "This whole thing has been surreal to watch. I never expected to be here."

"But you are." It's Corbin who speaks, causing both Olivia and I to look at him. "I bet everyone is really proud of you."

He doesn't mention our families, but I know it's who he means. "They are. All of them."

Olivia dismisses herself with a small wave before

heading over to a woman who shakes something in her hand at her.

"You were leaning forward," Corbin states quietly. "I always knew you were into a movie when you did that. Some things don't change, huh?"

I slide off the chair. "Some things do."

He turns and catches my wrist to stop me from walking away, quickly lowering his hand from mine before anyone sees. "Do you really believe what she said?"

"What do you mean?"

He sighs. "Don't play stupid, Little Bird. Do you believe you'll meet the right person again when the time is right?"

A humorless laugh bubbles out of me as I meet his gaze straight on. "I'm not the married one, Corbin. Maybe you should ask your wife."

I walk away in silence.

THE FAMILIAR NAME on my phone has me smiling as I walk to the car at the end of the day. There's no hesitation in answering like when other people call. I'm never too tired to hear from my brother.

"Hey, Gav."

"Dickwad," he greets.

Rolling my eyes, I laugh and mouth a quick *thank you* to the driver who's opening my door. Before I can climb in the back, my name is being shouted from across the lot.

"Who is that?" Gavin asks.

My eyes search the surroundings, but I don't know why. It isn't like I'm not familiar with the rasp of Corbin's voice by now. I've seen countless scenes, watched too many interviews, and I'm pretty sure I dream in the low gravelly tone that puberty has blessed him with.

No longer is the teenage boy encompassing the burly man that is Corbin Callum. It's almost like he doesn't want any piece of his old self embodied in the life he lives now. It's sad.

Knowing how Gavin feels about Corbin, I nibble my lip and watch as Corbin jogs over to where I sit with my feet still dangling out the car door.

All I get out is, "Uh…"

He deadpans. "It's *him*, isn't it?"

Lie. "No?"

Dropping my head back at the questionable answer, I listen to him curse over the line. "Please tell me the asshole isn't harassing you. It's bad enough you're working together—"

"That's a bit of a stretch," I cut it.

"Well, you have to see him every day."

"Not the same, but whatever." I debate on getting in and closing the door before Corbin can try talking to me, but something holds me back.

"I was checking to see how you're doing over in the big-leagues," Gavin redirects, though reluctant based on his mutterings.

"It's been an experience, but I'm okay." I want to ask him about the farm, the new barn renovation, and how my little nephew is doing. Unfortunately, I don't get to do that before Corbin is standing beside the car.

"Hey," he says, out of breath. "Glad I caught you. Mind talking for a minute?"

Gavin says, "Tell him no."

"Oh, shut up." I smile despite my brother's obvious distaste even after all these years, causing Corbin's brows to pinch. "Gavin is on the phone. I'll tell him you said hi."

"Tell him to fuck off," my brother replies.

I don't do that.

Corbin makes a face. "Uh, yeah. Hope he's doing okay."

The half-ass response is a worthy effort, but I can see something dulling his silver eyes. Instead of asking about it, I focus on my brother who's waiting for something to happen.

"Mind if I call you back in a few?"

He sighs heavily, in his typical overdramatic manner. "I see how it is. Some rich guy talks to you and you suddenly don't have time for the little folk."

His six-four height isn't what I classify as little, but I

know that's beside the point. "I'll call you back in two minutes. Stop being a diva."

"I need to get Little Man settled before I head off to do chores," he tells me, making my lips curve down. "We'll talk soon, sis. Punch the guy in the nuts for me, will ya?" He pauses. "On second thought, don't go anywhere near that general vicinity. Keep your distance."

"So, no dick punching?"

Corbin's eyes widen and I'm pretty sure his hand twitches to cover himself.

"Are there any rocks you can throw?"

"Go take care of my favorite nephew."

"He's your only—"

"Love you. Bye." Hanging up the phone, I shoot Corbin an innocent smile. "Gavin sends his love."

He blinks. "I can tell."

I shrug. "It sounded better than telling you to fuck off like he wanted. He hasn't changed much over the years. Except for the fact he's married and has a kid. Can you believe that? I still don't and Sam is almost two."

Realizing that I'm having mundane conversation with someone who I considered my enemy for a while, I zip my lips.

"That's ... wow. Gavin's a dad?"

I just nod.

"Huh." He rubs his arm. "Didn't really see him as

the settling down type, to be honest."

Snorting at the irony has him eying me knowingly. "Don't look at me like that, Corbin. You were the one who said that you'd never date. Now look at you."

He crosses his arms. "I recall breaking the no-dating thing not long after I said that. Or have you somehow blocked out your sophomore year?"

My eye twitches. "I'm unfortunate enough to remember everything. Thanks."

He looks away and sighs. "I didn't come over here to hash this out with you. We've established that I'm an asshole already."

My shoulder leans against the back seat as I study him closely. "What we haven't established is why. Why did you just up and leave without any contact? Tell me that and maybe I'll go easier on you."

His brows raise in disbelief. "Would you really though? I know you, Kinley. You hold on to anger to distance yourself from people. It's easier that way."

"You're stalling."

"Admit it."

I lean forward. "No."

He tips his head back. "It was pure selfishness. Is that what you want to hear? I found jobs that kept me on track to become what I am now and sacrificed everything to make a name for myself. I already told you that I chose me first. Happy now?"

I move my legs inside the car. "I'm happy that you

admitted it. But am I happy that I was never your prior-
ity? That everything we shared didn't matter to you like
becoming famous did? No, Corbin. I'm not."

"That's not—" He catches the door as I go to close
it. "That is not true. I know it doesn't seem like I gave a
shit, but I did come back."

My hand drops into my lap as I stare up at him with
a confused expression on my face. I would have known
if he came back. People talk. The local town gossip
would have made sure everyone in Lincoln knew if
someone who left reappeared one day, especially
someone like Corbin.

"Ask your brother."

I wet my lips and remain silent.

He opens the door and leans in, the woodsy scent he
smells like now nothing like the French vanilla that
surrounded him in high school. Weirdly, I miss it. "That
town is wrapped around your finger. It always has been.
As soon as I hurt you, I was the enemy. It doesn't
matter what award I win, or how much money is in my
bank account. Lincoln chooses you, which means they'll
protect you no matter what it takes."

I let him fill my personal space and invade my
senses before I close my eyes. "I don't think that's true."

"Then you're in denial, Little Bird."

"Please stop calling me that."

"Stop pretending like you still hate it."

Silence.

He stands up and flattens his shirt, gripping the edge of the door. "Meet me in my trailer tomorrow. We'll talk more. I'm not giving you a chance to say no either. We both need this."

"Closure?"

The infamous smirk appears on his face, leaving me wishing I did have a rock to throw at him. "The company."

I'm about to tell him that I can find better company than him, but he makes sure all my limbs are out of the way before closing the door. Staring at him through the glass, he shoots me a wink before turning around and walking away.

"What am I doing?" I whisper.

twelve

KINLEY / 16

BITING DOWN ONTO MY THUMBNAIL, I watch as the little white numbers in the bottom righthand corner of my laptop change. Eyes drifting to my inbox, I begin tapping my foot on the floor waiting for a new email to come through. The clock could be fast on my computer.

Noon.

12:01

12:05

12:09

A pillow smacks me in the face, and my laptop nearly topples from where it's perched on my legs.

Glaring at Gavin standing by the chair in the corner of my room, I put my laptop safely on my nightstand.

"Do you mind?"

"Your moping is annoying," he informs me, jabbing his thumb backwards. "Let's go get pizza. I'll even let you pay."

I blink.

He grins. "Come on, dickwad. I'm just messing with you. Although, feel free to pay. My milk check this week wasn't as much as I thought it'd be. You'll just have to live without your crack for now."

Rolling my eyes, I glance at the screen before sighing and closing my computer. "Fine, but you're definitely paying. *And* you're buying me Twizzlers because it's your fault I'm addicted to them in the first place."

He cackles and backs up. "Do you remember when I hit you with one during a road trip and you bruised?"

I throw the pillow back at him, but he catches it. "That hurt! Candy shouldn't be used as weapons."

"It was funny," the idiot says.

I get up and grab a hoodie before we walk downstairs. When Gavin grabs his truck keys, I slap them out of his hand. He complains when I inform him we're walking, since the gas station is right down the street.

We walk side by side, his broad frame taking up too much of the sidewalk and forcing me to walk partially on the grass along the road. He's taller and leaner than

Dad and likes to show off the biceps he's gotten from doing so much physical labor on the farm.

His shoulder bumps mine. "What were you obsessing over?"

Heat creeps into my cheeks. "Just a writing contest. It's stupid. They said the winners would be contacted at noon our time. I thought…"

I try not getting my hopes up when I enter contests. Since winning the first one, I've come in third and fourth place in two others. People tell me how much they love my writing samples and stories online. Some even say they can picture me getting published if I expand them into full length novels.

This contest is different though. I've been more confident in the story I wrote for it than any other sample I've submitted. Maybe it's because I based it on a silver-eyed boy and his best friend. Subconsciously, I know that it's stupid to write about something so close to me. The story flowed though — the love between a young Ryker and Beck growing which each story about them I write. It gives me hope. Hope for what, I'm not sure. But the feeling in my stomach when I'm around Corbin inspires me to write a story like ours.

But I jinxed myself by getting cocky after I landed in the final three for the judges to consider. The prize is another publication in a well-known magazine as well as a chance to speak to a literary agent about the process of being represented.

"Anyway, I didn't win."

Normally he'd make a sarcastic comment that would make me want to push him in front of a car, but instead he nods. "There are other contests, Kin. I know it sucks, but you'll win another one."

I told the entire family about the first competition I won over dinner one night. The conversation had lulled after talking about Gavin getting another calf from an auction he and our uncle went to, so I thought it was a good segue into letting them in on my good news.

Dad said, "Congratulations."

Mom said, "That's cool."

Gavin smiled at me from across the table.

The pride I'd felt for getting the story put into a magazine had dwindled by their lack of excitement. I try not to think about it, especially when Corbin tells me that my feelings are all that matter, but I care about what my family thinks. It's a fatal flaw.

I should have known that Gavin smiling was more than just an obligatory response. He doesn't tell me he's proud with words. It's in the way he smiles.

"You're right," I finally reply.

The gas station comes into view.

Gavin says, "Surprised you're not with your little boyfriend. You two spend a lot of time together."

Side-eyeing him, I notice his lips are pressed in a firm line. "Is that your way of trying to confirm we're dating?"

He eyes me skeptically. "Are you?"

I smile. "Corbin is my best friend. He isn't like anyone else at school. He has dreams that are a lot like mine."

"To write?"

"Act."

Gavin grunts. "Is he in drama club?"

Gavin and his friends used to make fun of drama club and the productions we'd sometimes be forced to watch during the school day. I get that the school wants to boost curiosity and get us to beg our families to come buy tickets and see the whole thing, but it never worked on my family. Mom and Dad both have busy jobs that make it difficult to do things after they get home.

"He'll be in the winter play," I confirm, not going into detail about what his role is. Thankfully the school isn't doing *Grease* again, but *Newsies* which is one of my favorites.

Gavin doesn't say anything, probably holding back the remark that's resting at the tip of his tongue.

"He got an acting coach," I blurt. When Corbin showed up at my house last week, I'd had a facemask on while sporting my ugliest pajamas ever. The shirt had a couple holes in it, the pants were baggy and unflattering, and the mask made my entire face green and hard to move.

After he finished laughing at me, he informed me that the classes he'd been going to for the past month got him noticed by one of the newer coaches. The guy was interested in meeting up with Corbin to talk about what he wanted to do with his life, so him and his mom spent an entire afternoon going over the details about what to expect if they had an agreement.

"What does that mean?" Gavin finally asks, holding his arm out in front of me as a car speeds by us at the intersection.

Pushing his arm down, I shrug. "It just means that he's finally doing something about becoming an actor. You know, learning the trade and stuff."

"Is he going to leave?"

My eye twitches. "Lincoln doesn't exactly have opportunities for actors, Gav. He'll leave eventually."

He doesn't say anything with words, but his solemn head bob makes my frown deepen. Why is he being so weird about it? Corbin won't live out his dream if he stays here.

I elbow his arm. "What?"

He shakes his head and opens the glass door for me that's littered with tobacco ads and two-for-one specials on soda. When I step through, I wait for him to say something. He doesn't meet my eyes as he walks over to the counter and orders our usual pepperoni pizza.

Guiding me over to where the big bottles of soda rest on the shelf, he grabs a Dr. Pepper and then gestures toward the candy section with his chin. "Nothing, Kin. Just grab your candy so you can't say I don't love you."

After he pays for everything, we sit at a table in back and wait for the pizza. "What are you thinking?"

He sighs and stretches his long legs out, ripping apart one of the napkins from the dispenser. "If you're just friends, it won't matter, but you've never had a guy friend before. You talk about him all the time. *Corbin this* and *Corbin that*. If he's going to leave..." His shoulders lift, then he looks up at me through thick lashes that he got from Mom. "Don't look at me like that. I just don't want to see you get hurt. By anyone other than me."

"I'm not staying here forever either," I point out, unsure of what else to say. He's insisting that more is going on with Corbin than there is. It'll be Christmas soon, which means the annoying cocky boy I was tasked to show around has been here for almost four months. It's true that we're always together, but nothing has ever happened that would warrant his suspicion about us being more than friends.

"But you're also not going to follow him around if he ever makes it," he counters, sitting forward and dragging his feet under his chair. "I just want you to see that your friendship with him may be great now, but it's not forever."

Now I roll my eyes at the thought of him trying to be all brotherly and protective. "I love you, Gavin, but there's nothing to warn me about. Corbin and I are just friends. I won't get hurt. One day, we'll both make lives for ourselves outside of Lincoln."

"And you'll be fine with that?"

"Why wouldn't I be?"

His silence is deafening.

The conversation dies into nothing but the sound of the woman making our pizza and the door opening with customers coming in to pay for gas and grab snacks.

I watch the stoplight flicker from yellow to red, and the cars turning despite the sign hanging on the line that tells them no turning right. Nothing ever stops anyone around here, and that gives me hope that everything will be okay.

Corbin will become a famous actor.

I'll become a famous writer.

We'll be happy.

ON CHRISTMAS EVE, the giddiness of the following day takes hold of the town. The glittery decorations hanging from the streetlights make the walk from the Tryon more festive along with the carolers singing in the square. Everyone is always happier this time of year, playing nice with their neighbors and smiling more. I never understood, but I like it.

I'm halfway down Main Street bundled in three different layers when headlights get nearer from behind me. The crunching snow under slowing tires has me

turning to see a white Jeep pulling over to the shoulder
of the road.

"Seriously?" Corbin says.

"Hey."

He rolls his eyes. "Get in."

Too cold to argue, I quickly make my way around
the front of the Jeep and climb into the passenger seat.
The cab is toasty warm, so I put my hands in front of
the vents and sigh in relief.

His scolding comes as expected. "I told you to call
me when you clocked out."

I lean back in the seat. "You told me you were
helping your mother run some last-minute errands
when we texted on my break. I figured you were
busy."

He hesitates before sighing, still not putting the car
in drive. "Dad came home early and helped her instead.
I was waiting for you to call me."

Corbin's relationship with his father still confuses
me, but it's not a topic he likes talking about. Mr.
Callum seems nice enough, but Corbin has mentioned
that he has anger issues caused by an accident he was in
a few years ago that makes him hard to be near for long
periods of time. Never knowing what to say, I just let
him change the subject when it comes up.

"I'm sorry," I murmur, resting my hands on my lap.

He shrugs and reaches for something in the back
seat. When he produces a green and red wrapped

present with a huge silver bow on it, a huge smile spreads on my face.

"Dad won't let me come see you tomorrow. Said I'd be bugging your family." He sets the gift on my lap. "But I wanted you to have your gift. Even wrapped it myself."

He says the last part so proudly, I can't help but laugh and poke at the bow. "The color matches your eyes."

"That's what Mom said."

I bite my lip. "Can I open it now?"

He taps the steering wheel. "Yeah, as long as your parents won't think you got kidnapped and call the cops."

I scoff and tear at the wrapping. "They know where to look first. I mean, if I'm not with you then there's definitely another strange man lurking outside of dark restaurants waiting for me. Sounds familiar…"

He flicks my arm. "Still not funny."

I stick my tongue out. "It is."

Once I finally get the wrapping off, keeping the bow intact so I can keep it, I stare down at the padded burgundy notebook in front of me. In golden script lettering, it says *most of all, let love guide your life.*

Running my fingers over the magnetic latch that keeps it closed, I flick it open and study the pretty cream pages with inspirational quotes on the top of each one.

"Corbin," I whisper.

"It's silly, but I figured you could use something new to write in," he tells me quickly.

Instead of answering, I lean forward and give his cheek a quick peck. When I settle back in my seat, I hug the notebook to my chest. "This is perfect. Thank you."

His lips part but nothing escapes them.

I reach into my pocket and pull out a piece of paper. My cheeks warm as I pass it to him, partially wishing I tried harder at finding something for him for the holiday.

He slowly takes it and glances down at the advertisement listed. "I found this when I was reading the paper. I know, I know. The paper is really lame, but if I hadn't been reading it, I wouldn't have seen the ad. You'd be perfect for what they're looking for."

The capital region tends to film a lot of commercials and made for TV movies. Although not many are well-known, locals are cast to involve the community. Corbin already spends a lot of time in the area because he takes acting classes there.

"It's a movie casting call," he says slowly, meeting my eyes after scanning the ad again. "Is this real?"

"Yes." I grin. "And you have an audition, so you better be on your A game because they're expecting the best."

He blinks.

I wait for a reply. "You okay?"

He shifts his body toward me. "How…?"

"I called your coach and told him about the ad. He already heard about it, of course, but he agrees that you'd do well. It's not the lead or anything, but it's a small role. Better than an extra, from what your coach said. And—"

"You really did that for me?"

I nod. "You want to act, and I want to support you. It's kind of perfect. You got me a gift that will help me keep writing, and I got you one that could lead to more acting. We're the perfect team."

He lowers the paper and stares at me until I'm squirming. *Why is he looking at me so weirdly?* The version of me that likes to overthink starts doing just that, until I'm regretting not getting him a funny t-shirt with his cat's face on it instead.

"Listen—"

"I love this," he states.

My regret vanishes. "Really?"

He lets go of the paper and leans over to give me a tight hug. I snuggle into him even though the console between us makes it hard and wrap my arms around his midsection. He rests his chin on the top of my head and we stay like that for a while without talking. We've been finding ways to touch more often—hug, lean against each other, any form of contact. I never think twice about it because it feels natural.

I feel his heartbeat against my chest and gnaw on the inside of my cheek at how it's racing. He moves back slightly, his warm breath caressing my parted lips. The tips of our noses brush, causing a little rack of shivers down my spine. I hear the faintest shift in his breathing and close my eyes as his face draws nearer.

The ghost touch of his hesitant lips over mine has my entire body heating. It lasts less than two seconds, but the impact is made. My lips tingle and my heart races and my skin pebbles. Swallowing and pulling back, I smile at him and pick up the notebook again.

He buckles and puts the car into drive before signaling to turn back onto the street. Wetting his lips, he says, "We're more than a perfect team, Little Bird."

Staring down at the notebook, I find myself taking a quiet breath. Neither of us speaks except to say goodnight.

thirteen

CORBIN / Present

THE CHAIR SETUP for me is right next to Kinley. I can feel her body heat as we watch the scene between Olivia and Aaron, who plays her fiancé, play out in front of us. From the corner of my eye, I notice the slightest part of Kinley's lips as she stares unblinkingly at Olivia and Aaron embracing in the middle of the room.

Her hands twitch on her lap as she watches Olivia wrap her arms around Aaron's neck. His hands rest on her waist, his forehead on hers, as he brushes her nose in a peck of his lips.

"What are we doing, Beck?"

Olivia tightens her hold on him. "Going back to what it was like before."

His response is delayed as he watches her, her eyes closed and her body melting into his in needed comfort. Then, his arms hook around her waist and hugs her to him. He sighs and rests his cheek on the top of her head, clear indecision featured on his pinched expression.

"Go back to what exactly?"

"When we were happy," she answers. It's so quiet that I almost miss it, but Kinley mouths the words so clearly that I can't help but study her instead of the couple in front of us.

I lean back in my chair and study Kinley's slumped posture, the same way she always sits when she can't stop watching something—a movie, a play, a scene. It makes me smile to myself knowing I can still see the old version of her inside the woman she's become.

When she turns my way and sees me staring, her cheeks blossom a light shade of pink. I just wink at her and turn back to Olivia and Aaron, pretending like I wasn't caught.

It's Aaron who caresses Olivia's cheek and says, "I'm not sure it's possible to go back that far, Beck. I know you've tried, but it's never been me as much as I wanted it to be."

Olivia withdraws, eyes widening.

Aaron smiles sadly. "I'll love you unconditionally like I promised I would when you gave us a chance, but we both know you want to take it back."

"Ian—" She steps back. "What…?"

His head tilts. "When the right person comes along, you don't have to work so hard to be happy. That's all you do though. Work. Happiness is just supposed to happen when you're with the person that's meant to be yours. It may not always be easy, but it's supposed to be more than this. I see it in your eyes, Rebecca. It's not me you want."

Olivia stares at the floor.

Aaron tips her chin up. The smile on his face is genuine as he brushes her bottom lip with the pad of his thumb. "This is on me too. I wanted to pretend we were meant to be something more. I know you and your heart. You wanted to give me that happiness, but it's not mine to have."

Olivia tries speaking but can't. A choked sob escapes her lips that Aaron tries comforting away by holding her close to him. She buries her face in his chest as he brushes his fingers through her hair.

"It's okay, Beck. I forgive you."

It takes her a moment, but she says, "You shouldn't. I'm a bad person, Ian. The things I've done…"

Aaron draws back and holds her face. "We all do

things we're not proud of to find the happiness that's just out of reach."

Olivia just stares.

Leaning in, Aaron kisses her cheek. "It was too easy for us, wasn't it? It's not supposed to be that way."

Finally, Olivia says, "No. It's not."

When the scene ends, Buchannan goes over and pats Aaron on the back and says something to Olivia that makes her smile. It gives me time to nudge Kinley's arm, getting her to turn her focus from them to me.

I smile. "I'm proud of you, Little Bird."

She blinks. "Thanks?"

Chuckling at her confusion, I rest my ankle on my opposite knee and lean back. "You congratulated me a while ago on living my dreams but look at you. Neither of us chose easy career paths, yet we still made it. I can tell how much this means to you." I gesture around us. "I see the way you mouth along with the lines and try wiping away tears before anyone can see you're emotional. You deserve to be though. Embrace it."

She looks away for a moment. "I'm not a fan of people seeing me emotional."

"Why?"

Her hand forms a fist and squeezes, before loosening her grip. "When you let your feelings be known, you're vulnerable. People look at you differently when they see you at your weakest. I know because I was there before."

My brows draw in. "Kinley…"

"Lincoln pities me," she informs me. "I get why you think they're on my side, but it's not like that. They see me as a heartbroken teenager who trusted a boy with big dreams. I decided to channel all those emotions into my work to get where I am. I'm lucky that there's a distraction for the town to focus on. That doesn't change how they see me though. I'll always be seventeen with puffy eyes, waiting for the day that the boy she loves shows back up."

I hear one thing. *Loves.* Present tense.

"Like I said. I forgive you, Corbin."

My eyes open to stare at her.

"I wouldn't be here without you." One of her shoulders lift and lowers as her expression turns sullen. "Kind of funny, huh? I made a career for myself because of you. I used to be so angry, but I should be grateful."

I shake my head, sitting up. "Don't be grateful for that. We both know I don't deserve the credit for what you put to paper."

She slides out of her chair and clicks her tongue. "Yet, here we are."

I purse my lips. "Yeah. Here we are."

Before she can walk away, I call out her name again. "You never came to my trailer the other day."

She hesitates. "Do you really think that's a good idea?"

All I can do is smile. "No," I admit. "But I'll make it worth it."

To my surprise, I see the faintest smile tip up the corners of her lips. And that's how I know there's hope for us. Because she'll show up.

fourteen

KINLEY / Present

THE SUN IS SETTING by the time I find the courage to walk over to the trailer with Corbin's name plastered on the door. It's nothing like I would expect a star's trailer to look like. It reminds me of my brother's first single wide that he proudly bought for himself shortly after moving away from home.

Taking a step back, I debate on what to do. I should be going back to the hotel and eating the leftover salad I ordered the night before. My laptop should be out with my current book pulled up to be written so I can submit it to my editor as agreed upon.

What I shouldn't be doing is this.

One deep breath later, I'm knocking on the door just below the lettering of his first name. I remember an old conversation we had about what his trailer would look like someday. Having his name on a door is like having mine on a book cover. It makes the dream more real.

When the door opens, my mouth goes dry at the sight of Corbin in blue jeans and a loose tee. It takes me a moment to pull myself together from all the times I'd see him wear this exact thing when we were younger. Long gone is the business wear that differentiates his two worlds.

"I was wondering if you were going to bail," he says by greeting. Half his lips quirk up at me as he steps aside. "Coming in or going to keep staring?"

Brushing it off, I straighten my shoulders and walk up the steps. Just as I pass him, his chest brushes my shoulder as he reaches behind me to close the door. He chuckles when I eye him suspiciously, then walks further into the trailer toward a little kitchen area.

"This is…" I take in how homey the inside is. There are a few counters with a microwave perched on one and a fridge next to it. The sink is on the opposite end, where the kitchen leads to a built-in wooden eating area. The benches are padded and clothed with black cushions and the table between them is the same wood as the counters and paneling.

"Wow," is all I remark.

As I'm turning to examine the rest of the space, I stop and stare at the large flat screen TV mounted on the wall in front of a huge black suede couch. The screen has *Carrie* displayed on it with the curser hovering over the play button.

Corbin comes up beside me. "It's the remake they did a few years back. Figured you probably hadn't seen it."

He's right, I haven't. Anything that reminded me of him I tried to avoid if I could help it. Since Stephen King was his obsession, it wasn't hard to do. I've only read a few books by him that Corbin got for me, and not another since.

"You wanted to be part of that film," I say quietly, walking over to the couch and seeing a closed pizza box on the wooden coffee table.

"It would have been cool," he agrees, sitting down on one end of the couch. "But I still plan on being part of other films based on his books. Plus, the cast for this is great."

I eye the spot nearest me, then look back at the assortment of food items littering the table. My gut tells me there's something familiar in the plastic bag, so I reach forward and peek inside.

"What are you doing?" I whisper.

"Going back."

My eyes widen. "Corbin—"

"Just sit down, Little Bird." He pats the cushion and picks up the remote. "We both need a break. What better way to do it?"

The Twizzlers, pizza, and soda take me back to the uneasy nervousness I experienced the very first time I hung out with him in his bedroom in that yellow house in Lincoln. It should be different now—the gut feeling settled into my stomach as I examine the man draped causally on the couch only feet from me. It isn't though.

Corbin was confident then, but that confidence is tenfold now. He has no reason not to be. His body is in pique condition, his career is huge, and he can get anything he wants with one little wink from those stupid melted lead eyes.

"You're not playing fair," I state, reluctantly taking a seat despite my better judgment egging me to leave.

The wafting scent of cheese and grease has my stomach growling. I haven't eaten since breakfast because I've been battling myself all day on should I or shouldn't I. Logically, the answer is obvious.

But here I am, losing a battle I had no chance at winning as soon as he stepped back into my life. I knew I'd wind up here eventually, pretending like nine years didn't separate us so we could live our own lives like nothing happened. As soon as my agent called to tell me the exciting news about the movie cast, it was all over.

When the movie starts, Corbin passes me a plate of pizza and tosses an unopened package of Twizzlers at me. Glaring at his innocent expression, I just focus on eating and watching the screen.

"You're not eating any of this?" I ask when he leans back without getting himself any.

"Not really in the diet plan."

I roll my eyes. "I'm not eating all this on my own, superstar. Don't you have some overpriced trainer to get you to do a few extra sit-ups for occasions like this?"

His laugh is deep, causing little goosebumps to pebble my arms. "Suppose you're right. I don't have a shirtless scene tomorrow, so I guess I can indulge."

Shaking my head, I don't bother remarking on how one slice of pizza won't harm his chiseled physique. The last thing he needs from me is a compliment about his body. Then he'd know I've most definitely been looking.

We're halfway through the movie when I decide to tuck my legs under me and settle into the small decorative pillow on my side. The Twizzlers on my lap have been dug into, and a few even thrown in the general direction that Corbin is sitting.

After getting comfortable, I freeze when a warm hand caresses my calf. My head lifts to see Corbin's eyes on the screen but his hand kneading absentmindedly at the tight muscles in my legs. I tell myself to move away or tell him to stop, but all I do is watch.

Swallowing, I try resting back down and watching the movie. A few minutes later, he extends my legs straight to drape them across his lap. His fingers work their magic on the other leg, before his palm drifts down to my socked feet. I unintentionally moan when he starts massaging them one at a time, leaving my eyes growing heavy from the relaxing sensation.

"You probably shouldn't do that," I say quietly, half sleep ridden.

"Probably," he agrees.

"I shouldn't be here."

"No?"

Keeping my eyes closed, I shake my head and listen to the movie. "We both know I shouldn't. Your wife..." My throat hurts and tears threaten to spill suddenly from my eyes. "I don't know why I'm doing this to myself."

His hands stop moving. "Lena and I aren't ... we're a bit complicated to explain, Kinley. The public doesn't really understand situations like ours."

I can't help but laugh dryly. There's a line in my book between Ryker and Beck that sounds an awful lot like this. You can't always predict when your story becomes relatable, but somehow, I walked right into this narrative.

Literally.

"How's that?" I play along.

To my surprise, his hands begin moving again as he explains. "Lena comes from a very traditional family. When we started dating, things got serious fast. Expectations were heavy despite our careers pulling us in different directions, but we both wanted more."

I won't lie and say it hurts to hear him talk about the woman he married. A woman who isn't me. Nobody wants to hear about how their ex moved on, complicated relationship or not.

"We rushed into a marriage that neither of us second guessed because we thought it was what was best," he continues softly. With my eyes still closed, I wonder if he's looking at me or staring at the TV hoping he won't see the crushed expression on my face. "Her family helped plan the wedding and in no time we were saying our vows. Things got … intense. Between work, married life, you name it. We've barely spent more than a few months together in the years we've been married. Our jobs keep us busy. We try making it work and meeting up when we can, but it isn't that simple. This year we decided it may not be worth the hassle."

My entire body locks up.

"But like I said. Her family is traditional."

Now I'm hyperaware of the conversation we're having. My eyes open but stay focused in front of me instead of at the man who's divulging secrets that clearly nobody else knows. Wetting my dry lips, I try evening my heartbeat that's racing from the unknown.

"Lena can't get divorced without repercussions from her family. She's worried about what they'll say when they find out it didn't work out between us. Her father is strict, her mother tried getting her to reconsider from the beginning. It..."

I hold my breath.

"It wasn't my biggest mistake in life," he admits, blowing out a breath. "Because Lena is what I needed for a while. She became something I could focus on without looking back. I'm a selfish man for that, but it wasn't any different for her. We clicked, had some things in common, but it wasn't meant to work out."

I ask, "How do you know?"

"Because we could have tried harder to make it work and decided not to," he answers instantly. "This project has meant more to me than I realized it would. I knew I wanted to be on it as soon as my agent told me it was an adaptation of your book, Kinley. Being able to see you again? Bring something you did to life? It just felt like something I needed to be part of."

I sit up and stare at him.

He shrugs and looks at me. "What I didn't realize at the time was that this story is beyond you and me. It started out as a way to have you in my life again when I thought I needed the opposite in order to stop thinking about you. But then I read the script and I realized that Lena and I are no different than Beck and Ian. We both settled for a happiness we thought we could achieve while pining for other things. This industry feeds off failed relationships, so normally a divorce would only be front page news for a day before the next scandal happened. It isn't like that for her and me though."

I try wrapping my head around what he's saying. "Are you really staying married to someone you don't love because of what other people will think?"

"Kinley, it's not that simple."

"When I wrote Beck and Ian's storyline, I did it because I wanted to show that some people felt like settling was their punishment for the things they did in the past." I draw my legs in and wrap my arms around my bent knees. "Beck blames herself for not loving Ryker the way he wanted her to when they were younger. She chose to move on and experience what it's like to live and date and get attention from other people. You know what she felt?"

"Lonely," he answers audibly.

I nod once. "Yes. Lonely. Beck knew how much Ian loved her which is why she thought she could find that same love for him as time passed. Why wouldn't she? He's a kind, supportive, caring person. In every way, they're perfect for each other. But she knows that there are other people meant for them—not just how Ryker has always been meant for her, but that some lucky girl out there is meant for Ian. Settling for people that you think you can be happy with just means taking away other people's happiness."

"Why?"

I blink. "Why what?"

"Why would Beck blame herself for not loving Ryker from the start? Any logical person would want what she did. Anyone would choose to go out and live their lives instead of being saddled with someone as intense as Ryker."

"That's not how love works, Corbin."

He cocks his head. "Then tell me how it works. Explain it to me, Little Bird, because I'm clearly not following. You say that love is painful and nearly impossible to find. You believe that there's a right time and place for everything, and that if it doesn't work out then that's all there is to it. What happens then?"

My lips part ... then close.

"I'll tell you what," he says, grabbing my leg and pulling me forward. I yelp when my butt grazes his thigh and his hand grips one of my legs while the other awkwardly spreads to make room for his body as he leans forward.

"Corbin—"

"We fuck up. Over. And over. And over." He twists his body so he's between my thighs, hands resting on other side of my torso as he hovers over me. "You said it best. We'll keep making mistakes because we don't want to learn. Are you going to deny that you haven't thought about us? Felt anything for me? Remembered what it was like when we were together?"

My hands shake as they find his chest, but I don't have the energy to push him away like I mean to. "Are you really asking me that? I'm not the one who walked away! *You* are. Don't ask me stupid questions about if I remember what it was like because you know I do. You know how much it hurts that there's not one thing I've forgotten. It fucking haunts me, Corbin. How much I gave to you, expected from you, it hurts so bad that I want to rip my heart out until it's clean of you."

"Windows of opportunity open and close all the time in this industry," he tells me without any real emotion spattered across his face. "If you stop for even a second then you become irrelevant."

I'm not sure why he says that. "You've never been irrelevant, Corbin."

His hand brushes my cheek. "Not to you, Little Bird. Never to you. But the world I threw myself into? That's different. If I called you sooner, came home sooner, I would have had nothing to show for leaving in the first place."

My lip quivers. "And you do now?"

His brows furrow. "Do you not see what I've built for myself? The name? The movies? The deals? I'm exactly where I want to be in this business. It's everything outside my career that I want to change. So, what do you mean?"

"The way I see it," I say slowly, "the only thing you have that truly matters is a marriage certificate to a woman you don't even love. I'd like to think the Corbin

I knew back then wouldn't have sacrificed *that* much for an image he can't even change if he wanted to."

This time, he doesn't answer.

My fingertips dig into his cotton shirt, bunching it as I clench a fistful in my hands. "I have been in failed relationship after failed relationship because I've never been able to get over you. I've had to see pictures of you on magazines in stores holding your wife's hand and kissing her and hugging her while I buy food for one because guys realize I'm not worth the complication. I've let myself down for loving you and the worst part is…"

Don't say it.

"I can't seem to stop." I choke out the last word through the tears that trail down my cheek.

His throat bobs as he brushes them away, his own eyes looking nothing like the bright silver the world is used to admiring. The dark tones are pits of agony that I know are reflections of my own.

Then … it happens.

The years of separation.

Of anger.

Of heartache.

Everything that's left me buried in work just so I don't have to think about the boy who left me behind comes crashing down.

The lips on mine are familiar yet foreign, soft but hard, searching and needing. He leans into me until our bodies are pressed together and a satisfying weight settles on top of me as his mouth and teeth and tongue bring me back to a time when we fumbled and laughed and worked our way through every kiss. He wasn't a virgin when we met and knowing that back then killed me a little. Sabrina Christy was a name I'd have engraved in my head when he admitted she was his first —some old classmate at the last school he was in. I envied her ability to have something I couldn't while he took the very same thing from me when I offered it.

And now his experience is obvious. Corbin Callum knows what he's doing. My bet is he's had plenty of practice since the days of fumbling with bra hooks and cursing at leggings.

I want to hate him for it—for having so much experience when the amount of men I've let in my life since him is so minimal. Yet, I can't find myself to feel anything other than desire and yearning and guilt, all wrapped up into one.

His tongue tastes and twists with mine, and I drink him in every time he angles his head for a deeper kiss. My arms wrap around his neck as my pelvis arches into his until I feel something deliciously hard brush against my inner thigh.

"Fuck," he curses, moving his lips down my neck and his hands down my body. I'm panting and writhing and wanting and hating myself more and more by the second.

The heat gathering between my thighs becomes so intense that I'm afraid I'll combust right here on the spot. It outweighs the reason that screams at me to stop before I make a huge mistake. I do what I've never done before. I guide his hand down my stomach until he's cupping me where I need him most.

The groan he awards me with comes with the slightest twitch of hardness that I know is trapped uncomfortably in his jeans. But he doesn't move to undo the button and zipper like I want him to. Instead, he reaches for the waistband of my leggings and pulls them down until they rest just above my knees.

His eyes flare. "You're not wearing any panties."

Slightly embarrassed but too turned on to really care, I just shake my head and dig my fingernails into his arms.

"I've got you, Little Bird."

I'm not sure what he means until his head dips down and his mouth covers the most sensitive part of me. My hips jerk up as he licks and sucks the bundle of nerves before sliding his tongue down the length of my slit and tasting me from bottom to top.

"C-Corbin." My grip on him has to hurt, maybe even draw blood, but I don't care. He keeps working me with his mouth until his tongue pierces my opening and moves in and out while his nose brushes my clit in a torturous rhythm.

My legs widen as far as they can with my leggings

still wrapped around my knees, giving him more access to sink into me. Shakily, my fingers weave into his hair and pull as I start feeling a familiar tingling in the pit of my stomach as my movements become jerky.

Mentally, I tell myself to stop enjoying it. Internally, I scream to end this moment between us before it goes too far. But my brain and heart want two different things, and I can't stop the battle inside my body. I'm at war with my morals and have nowhere to go.

I torture myself for staying away.

I torture myself for keeping him close.

I'm trapped between right and wrong.

"That feels so good." I cover my face with the crook of my arm and moan out his name as he focuses on my clit again while using a finger to get me off quicker.

Stop this, my inner voice demands.

But I ignore her.

My legs tighten around his head as I come, my moans becoming incoherent and breathy. He keeps sucking me until my body goes completely still from the numbness of an intense orgasm I haven't felt in far too long.

Closing my eyes, I catch my breath and try not to think about the sound of his zipper moving down and the ruffling of denim shifting against perfect skin.

"Please," he whispers. "I need you."

When I look at him, his eyes are wide and glazed

over with lust and something else. Something I told myself is impossible to see in eyes like his.

Love.

And, for a moment, I wonder if the reason I haven't been able to let go is because I'm not supposed to. Like maybe this is meant to be something worth fighting for no matter the circumstances. But how far would I have to go?

My head slowly nods as his hands go back to my leggings to peel them off the rest of the way. I help him shed his shirt, then take off mine, until there's limited clothing separating us. The tented front of his boxer briefs have me itching to reach out and touch him, but he shakes his head like he knows what I want.

I've always remembered our first time, and the times after, no matter who I was with. The first man I let into my bed following Corbin had to deal with my break-down following the sex that left him redressing in record time before making an excuse to leave.

"You're gorgeous," he tells me, kissing me while lining himself up at my center. The taste of me on his lips shows how much we've changed. No longer does he hesitate but dominates. He knows how to work my body and give me everything I'm too afraid to ask for.

I suck in a breath as he enters me inch by inch, his lips teasing mine as he stretches me out.

My lids flutter closed as he nips my chin, my jaw,

and my neck as his hands move to grip my hips. His fingernails dig into my bare skin as his pace picks up.

"Do you remember this?" he asks, licking an area on my neck where he bit. He changes angles that hits me deeper, harder, and faster. "I remember. I couldn't keep my fucking hands off you then. You've always been so beautiful."

Tears well that I can't explain. I kiss him as a distraction from the feelings weighing down my chest, holding onto him as his hips drive into me in a way he never used to before.

Burying my face in his neck, I brush kisses along his collarbone and moan as he hits me in just the right spot. Eyes rolling in the back of my head, I hold onto him tighter. My gaze meets two little marks that I never thought I'd see again. Tracing the lines on his pec, I remember the very first time he showed me what he'd done. The tattoo was still red and puffy then, but I'd touched him just as I did now. He told me the lines represented us, two entities equal to each other. But I could tell just by looking into his eyes that there was more to the story—something he wasn't willing to share. And like always, I let him have his secret.

I begin saying something when his phone starts ringing. He ignores it, grabbing onto my hips and grazing my ass to pump harder into me. When I try moving to see who's calling, he kisses me with everything in him. It's how I know whose name is lighting up his screen.

"Corbin—"

"Don't," he pleads, his cock hardening in me as he lays me back down and fucks me harder.

Because that's what this is.

Fucking.

Screwing.

Nothing more.

The tears that well now make their way down my cheeks as he buries his face in my neck and thrusts a few more times before reaching between us and playing with my clit.

"Don't," I tell him, stopping his hand.

He sits up on his arms and slows his movements, brows pinching. "Kinley…"

"Just finish."

"Kinley—"

"Just fucking come, Corbin!" I hiss, grabbing onto his shoulders and kissing him with a ferocity that has him stunned as he begins moving again.

Harder and harder and harder.

Until—

"*Fuck.*" He pulls out just as he comes, hot stickiness hitting the inside of my leg while I stare at how his chest rises and falls.

His phone starts ringing again.

I dare to look. Because I hate myself. Because I need to punish myself like Beck does.

Swallowing, I say, "You should probably answer that."

Sitting up, I grab his discarded shirt from the floor and wipe myself off before collecting my clothes that are scattered everywhere.

"Kinley," he whispers, not picking up the cell that so blatantly displays Lena's name.

I wave it off. "It's not like I didn't know."

And that's the problem.

Because I'd do it again.

fifteen

KINLEY / 16

MIDWEEK I'M HUDDLED up in the library with my new favorite notebook in front of me. My hand is grasping a test with a big red letter circled on the top that I'm not accustomed to seeing. Setting it down next to the story I've been writing in Earth Science, I realize there shouldn't be any surprise as to why I failed.

When a familiar pair of fancy sneakers comes into view, I look up at Zach just as he sits down next to me. His eyes go to my exam. "Shit." He winces and sits back. "I didn't do well either in that class. Surprised you're struggling. The way Corbin talks…"

I blow out a breath and shove the test inside my notebook before closing it. "Corbin gives me too much credit. Anyway, how are you two? Have things been okay?"

My eyes scan over the faded shiner. He and Corbin got into a fight over a week ago. When I heard about it from some girl in the hall, I confronted Corbin and asked if it was true. He hadn't shown up at my house to help me study the day it happened, and the puffy nature of his knuckles told me why.

I learned quickly that boy fights are nothing like girl ones. Apparently, Zach made a comment about Corbin's role in the school play. The rehearsals have been almost every day since Christmas break ended because the first show is set to premiere right before Valentine's Day. When Corbin admitted he'd hit Zach for giving him crap about it, I didn't believe him. But Zach didn't confirm or deny anything when I asked him.

"Yeah, Kin. We're good," Zach muses, throwing one foot up on the tiny table between us. "So, what's the deal with the test?"

Biting down on my inner cheek, I give him a limp shrug. "I haven't been paying attention, it's my fault."

He watches me for a second before pulling his water bottle out from the side of his bag next to him. "Is that why you're sulking in here? Pretty sure Corbin was looking for you."

Everyone knows that Corbin and I are joined at the

hip. Ever since the sort-of kiss on Christmas Eve, things have been strange. Neither of us have brought it up when we hangout, but we find ourselves holding hands or using each other as pillows during movies or study sessions. It's like we decided silently to pursue something without any conversation.

"What are *you* doing here?" I ask skeptically. Zach already told me he isn't a fan of books, which led to me jokingly tell him we couldn't be friends. Given he's still around, he didn't take the threat seriously.

He stuffs the bottle between his thigh and the side of the chair. "I was over by the computers playing games when I saw you moping."

"I'm not moping!"

He tilts his head and raises his brows.

I sigh. "Okay, maybe a little. I never fail anything. I've always done well in school, but I can't blame anyone but myself. I never even studied for this stupid exam."

"So, study next time," he states simply.

Realistically, it is as easy as that. All it takes is an hour a day the week leading up to an exam to get the material down. I've done it plenty of times before, but now my focus is on anything but school.

Despite that, I say, "You're right," and study the oncoming students walking to the side exit. Their jokes and giggles make me smile and miss Corbin. It's a weird feeling to miss someone you see often, and I'm not sure

I like it. When I wake up, I think about him. Before bed, I think about him. It's easy to channel that when I'm writing about Ryker and Beck because I want them to be realistic—conflicted and confused and happy and awkward. It seems to be exactly what Corbin and I are. Like we want to be something more but don't know how.

Zach tosses a balled-up piece of paper at me, but it bounces off my knee and lands on the floor. "You going to the game tomorrow night?"

The muffled snort that comes out of my mouth makes him laugh. "Uh, no. You remember how I said sports aren't my thing like reading isn't yours?"

His puppy dog look is better than any other I've seen, but it still doesn't work. "You won't even come to support your favorite player? Come on, Kinley, don't do me like that."

"She won't be doing you at all, Russo," a new voice says coolly from behind my chair.

Turning, I see Corbin staring at me. I wiggle my fingers at him. "Hey. I figured I'd see you later."

Corbin's eyes go to Zach and something flashes in them, but before I can ask what, he glances back at me with a blank expression. "A few people said they saw you here. Figured I'd bring you lunch since you skipped again."

"I didn't skip…" In fact, I can still taste the peanut butter from the sandwich I'd eaten in the computer lab.

I almost got yelled at by the teacher who's a stickler about eating by the computers but hauled butt out of there before he could even open his mouth.

Corbin's hand goes to my shoulder, squeezing it once. "What are you guys talking about anyway?"

"She won't come to the game."

Corbin probably rolls his eyes, but I'm not really paying attention. "You'd have better luck asking her to give up sugar."

My nose scrunches. "Not true."

Zach smiles. "You'll come then?"

"Nope."

He frowns.

Corbin laughs and let's go of me. "She'll be busy, Russo."

Now I do meet his eyes. "I will?"

His nod is terse. "I was going to ask you to run lines with me. Figured we'd talk about it on the way home."

Part of me perks up, but another notices the weird pinch to his lips. Collecting my things, I stand up and give Zach a small smile. "I'll consider going to a game … eventually."

The friendly jock smirks. "Before I graduate?"

"Eh…" I try to look like I'm really contemplating it, then stick my tongue out at him. "We'll see."

He waves me off with an amused grin, with Corbin hot on my heels as we leave the library. "You know he likes you, right?"

I scrunch my nose. "What? Who?"

Corbin glares. "Who do you think?"

I shake my head, moving hair out of my face that keeps falling into my eyes. "Don't be stupid. Zach and I are friends."

He grumbles something under his breath that I can't quite make out. "You down for running lines tomorrow? I think I have most of them memorized but wouldn't mind somebody to go through them with me before the audition. My coach found another one to practice for too. The auditions are on the same day."

My hand instantly goes to his wrist. "I'd love to help you! What is it for?"

"Commercial," he evades.

When he doesn't make a move to explain, my mind tries figuring out if I've seen any ads in the paper. Nothing comes to mind, so I jab his side to try getting something out of him.

"Is it embarrassing?" I laugh at the prospects that has him blushing right now. "Oh my God, it is! Are you representing a new hemorrhoid cream? Is it for an STD?"

He groans loudly and pushes me gently away from him. "Would you quit it? It isn't for anything like that. I just don't want to jinx it."

"I'll find out tomorrow," I remind him.

"Good," is all he replies with.

Frowning, we walk the rest of the way to our

lockers in silence. It gives me a chance to think about what he said earlier. Zach doesn't like me as anything more than a friend. Right? We tease each other a lot, but so do Corbin and me. It isn't that out of the ordinary.

Shoulders dropping, I loosen a sigh. "Do you really think Zach likes me? Like … *likes* me likes me. Because I don't get that vibe from him. Unless he said something to you…"

I lean against the locker next to his as he digs through his bag for who knows what. "Is that what you want?"

His tone is dry as he side eyes me.

"For him to like me? I don't know."

"You don't know," he murmurs, slamming his locker closed.

We stand face to face, him looking like he's about to bust a vein in his head. "What's your deal? It's not like I said I want to date him. I just want to know why you think that."

"It's…" His nostrils twitch. "He just looks at you like he does, okay? I'm a dude, I know this shit. So, do you?"

Did I miss the question?

He sees the confusion on my face. "I know you're not that familiar with guys liking you, but—"

"What is that supposed to mean?" It isn't like he's wrong, but his tone is making it sound like nobody could ever possibly like me as more than a friend.

He starts walking, leaving me to quicken my pace until I match his steps. "I'm just saying that you don't have experience with guys. It isn't surprising that you can't see he's flirting with you all the time."

"He does not—" I stop myself, trying to think to all the conversations I've had with Zach over the past few months. "He asked if I was going to the game. I'd hardly call that flirting."

Corbin halts and stares at me with distant eyes, as if to silently say, *are you that dumb?*

"Right?" My voice is tiny.

He swipes a palm across his face. "My bet is that he asked because he wants you there cheering him on. He never asks me if I'm going."

"Yeah, but you..." *Never go.*

He nods slowly. "Exactly. He's willing to get you to go because he wants to impress you. I don't get hounded because he doesn't want to get in my pants."

My lips part. "Wow. Crude, much?"

"It's true."

"He doesn't like me."

"He does, Little Bird."

We start walking again, and I soak up the information that he's dealing me. I mean, it wouldn't be the end of the world if Zach had a crush on me. Just ... foreign. Despite the embarrassment of acknowledging that I have zero experience with guys, I don't want to think I'm totally clueless.

But the more I think, the more I realize that's exactly what I am. Zach never goes to the library because it's the last place he's interested in. There are two different computer labs he could have used to play computer games in, yet he came to the smallest lab the library has set up for typing classes after school.

"Huh," I mutter, earning me a look from the corner of Corbin's eye.

We remain silent the rest of the day.

MY EYES GO to the script in front of me.

"You're kidding, right?"

He grumbles as I make myself comfortable on the edge of his bed. Fred is purring beside me, nuzzled up with one of Corbin's hoodie drawstrings next to him. I scratch his head and coo at him while Corbin settles in his computer chair across from me.

"This is for a dating app." I giggle, flipping through the few pages in front of me. "I don't get why you're even auditioning."

His sigh is heavy. "Daniel told me it'd be a good idea to keep my options open at first. If the other audition doesn't work out…"

"Hey, I get it." I give him a reassuring smile and hold up the script. "It just seems weird that you'd want to do this kind of thing. Can't he find other auditions for movies or something?"

"He said he would when I'm eighteen."

"That sounds promising."

"It's also forever away."

I deadpan. "You'll be eighteen in July. That's not even seven months from now. Plus, you mentioned anything helps with your portfolio, right?"

He just shrugs.

"If you get this part, everyone will want to use this dating app," I inform him confidently.

It's really no wonder his coach thinks he'd be perfect for it. He's young, but doesn't look like a teenager, and he's attractive. Hot, even, not that I'd tell him.

One of his brows goes up. "Yeah?"

I pet Fred some more. "Don't act like you don't know you're attractive. It's the eyes."

The two silver orbs light up.

I shake my head and lift the script. "You ready to go through this?" My eyes catch on the movie script next to him on the desk. "What if you end up getting both? Could you do the commercial too? You know, get the credit for it or whatever?"

He toys with the paper on his lap. "It'd depend on what the contract says. Some people don't like you working on more than one project at a time."

I frown. "That's stupid."

"We shouldn't focus on that anyway," he murmurs, scanning over the lines. "I might not get either. I didn't get the last few."

"Don't do that." If I had a pillow in reach, I'd smack him with it. How many times has he pulled me from my pity party after another contest was lost? Too many.

"I'm just being—"

"Stupid."

"—realistic," he finishes slowly.

I cross my arms on my chest. "When I called you crying over another one of my stories being turned down online, what did you tell me?"

His lips twitch. "To eat your feelings?"

I glare. "Before that, dummy."

Now he smirks. "That your time is coming, you just have to wait for the right people to see your talent."

My brows go up in reply.

"Yeah, yeah." He leans back and scrapes both palms down his face. "I'm just worried that I may be putting too much energy into something that won't happen."

"Says who?"

He doesn't answer.

"Corbin! Says. Who?"

"My dad, okay?" He blurts, looking toward his door. Getting up, he softly closes it and then leans his back against the wood. "He was having a moment and told me that I should think practically. Mom tried telling him that I'm good at what I do, but Dad brought up how I've just wasted gas money going to different auditions."

Wow. "That's ... I'm sorry."

"He never used to be like this." He pushed off the door and grabbed his script before laying down on the other side of Fred. "The car accident he got into a few years ago made him a different person. He always had some anger issues that Mom would get upset over, but hitting his head made it ten times worse."

My heart aches for him. "He doesn't, like, hit you guys or anything. Does he?"

"No. Nothing like that." He grabs ahold of Fred and sets him on his chest. "He'll lose it and yell over stupid shit or hit the walls. Mom had to plaster the hallway of our old house shortly after he got home from the hospital. He found out he had to do physical therapy before he could be cleared for work and lost it. He was stressed because Mom wasn't working, and bills couldn't be paid on time."

He pauses and lets Fred's purrs fill the silence between us. After a long moment, he adds, "That's why we moved here. It was kind of the start of the end. Some companies cut us slack until Mom could find a part time job to start paying things again, but Dad couldn't get cleared in time. The bank threatened to take our house if we didn't find a way to pay the mortgage. My grandparents offered to help, but Dad refused.

"Mom found a fulltime position at a local hospital that also had programs Dad could attend while he healed. It got him out of the house and got him to talk out his frustrations instead of punching more holes into the drywall."

I reach over and take his hand. I only planned on squeezing it, but he interlocks our fingers and keeps them resting on his stomach. Not knowing what to say, I just lean against the wall and let him process whatever he's thinking.

"Mom managed to get her parents to help pay the bills, but not long after that she lost her job. The grant that paid her and a few others was defunded, so they let them all go. Dad had just finished his PT only to find out another contractor got hired to finish his job because the people who hired him couldn't keep waiting. Dad found a job out here and the rest is history. He still has his moments. He punched the wall downstairs after we moved in because the movers were late. Mom and I patched it up and repainted it to try matching the color."

Nibbling on my lip, I stare at our hands and then glance at his face. One arm is bent behind him like a pillow as he stares up at the ceiling.

"I'm sorry your family has been through so much. For what it's worth, your Dad doesn't mean anything by it. It sounds like there's something wrong with how he processes things. Plus, it's a parent's job to worry about their kids. Mine aren't exactly keen on going with a career that can leave me homeless if a book flops."

His head turns to me. "I know you're right. It just ... sucks. But who knows? Maybe I'll get one of these parts and finally be able to tell him about it."

"He'll be proud," I agree.

He doesn't seem so sure.

We stay like that for a while longer, our hands joined and Fred soaking up the attention we both give him.

It's him who breaks the silence. "Can I ask you something?"

"Of course."

He hesitates. "Have you thought about what I said yesterday? About Zach?"

Internally, I groan. "Not really. I still don't think you're right about him liking me. It doesn't really matter anyway."

"Why not?"

I lay on my side and face him. "I don't like him like that. To me, we're just friends. It isn't like we talk that much, and we only ever hang out if you're around. I don't know him that well."

He doesn't say anything.

"Why does it bother you so much?"

"It doesn't," he quickly responds.

I roll my eyes. "You're a bad liar, Corbin. You get all short tempered when he's brought up. Ever since he commented on your acting, it's been weird between you two."

Again, no comment.

I flick his arm. "What's going on?"

"Nothing."

I sit up. "Let's just run lines. I'm not in the mood to be lied to, especially not by my best friend. Friends don't do that."

He sits up abruptly, causing Fred to launch off him and onto floor. "That's what is wrong, Kinley. The friend thing."

My chest tightens. Instantly, I think about the peck like kiss. Did it ruin everything? Make us weird? "What? If this is you saying you don't want to be friends any—"

"I want to be more than that," he cuts me off, pushing the script off the bed and swinging his legs over the side. "I swear, you're so dense for being so smart."

All I do is blink.

He stands up and turns around. "Zach and I didn't get into a fight because he talked shit about me. He was being egged on by some of the guys after gym to ask you out. Said he's been wanting to for a while. When I heard that..."

My jaw drops in shock. "You punched him over that?"

"I punched him because he was playing the cool guy in front of his other friends and it pissed me off."

"So ... you punched him?"

He throws his hands up. "Yes. Okay? Yes, I punched him. But you weren't there. He always thinks he needs to play the part in front of other guys. I don't doubt that he likes you, but he made it seem like you were head over heels and chasing him around like a puppy dog."

Jerking back, I shake my head. "That doesn't sound like something he'd do. Zach is a good guy."

"Around us," Corbin agrees.

My shoulders slump.

"I didn't want to tell you this way," he grumbles, pacing next to the bed.

"Tell me...?"

He stops and slowly turns to me. "Are you really going to make me say it?"

I just smile.

He locks eyes with me. "I like you, Kinley. You understand what it's like to want something so bad it hurts. You encourage me to keep going, you get my eagerness for auditions, you're just a good person. Sometimes I don't think I deserve you in any form—friend or not."

"Don't be stupid."

"I'm being honest." He sits back down on the edge of the bed, his knee brushing mine. "I don't want you to like Zach because I want you to like me. I'm selfish."

"I don't like Zach," I remind him.

"Does that mean you like me?"

"Is that even a real question?"

He waits.

"Yes." It comes out a whisper.

"Yeah?"

I roll my eyes and push his shoulder. "I just said that, what else do you want? What happened over Christmas ... I don't just let anyone do that."

He wets his bottom lip. "Speaking of, I can think of one thing I wouldn't mind doing again."

My eyes widen when he begins leaning toward me. I start thinking about the books I've read about kissing and how everyone seems to be instantly good at it. The last time doesn't feel like it counted as a first kiss. It happened so fast that I couldn't think about what to do or how to feel or freak out about my inexperience. I never understood why everyone in books and movies made it look easy.

Just before his lips brush mine, knuckles tap on the door and we both jerk away from each other. Mrs. Callum's voice cracks through the sound of my wild heartbeat as she opens the door and looks at us.

Corbin is holding his script and playing it off, while I just stare wide-eyed and silently thanking her for interrupting what I assume would have been an epic fail on my part.

"No closed doors with Kinley over," his mother reminds him.

Corbin's face turns red. "Mom."

She smiles at me. "Hi, dear."

"Hi, Mrs. C."

She looks at Corbin again with a warning eye before walking away with the door open. Corbin clicks his tongue and starts laughing.

I can't help but join in.

When we settle down, he takes my hand in his again. Staring at our hands in awe of how good they feel woven together, I say, "Corbin?"

"Yeah, Little Bird?"

"I'm not good at this."

He drags me back, lowering us down so my head uses his chest as a pillow. "I'm not either. We'll make it work."

I swallow my nerves. "Have you done this sort of thing before? You know, dated? Kissed? That ... stuff."

His momentary pause makes my body drown with disappointment. It's a personal question that I feel like I should know the answer to, but it feels weird to ask. I've always assumed he's been a lady's man considering the attention he gets from girls at our school. It's really no surprise. Anyone would be stupid not to like him.

"Yeah," he whispers, "I have."

My heart pings with pain. Sitting up, I look down at him with my bottom lip sucked into my mouth. "I haven't done anything. I'm new at all of this. What if it's awkward or I mess up? I don't want you to think—"

He cuts me off. "Stop, Kinley. Look at me, okay? We don't have to do anything you're uncomfortable with. Just because I've done some stuff before doesn't mean I'm going to force you to do anything. You know me better than that."

I know I shouldn't ask, but I do. "When you say that you've done stuff, do you mean…"

Palming his face, he nods. "Would it help if I told you about it? Believe me, Little Bird. It wasn't that special. It involved drinking and the backseat of a car. Not my finer moment."

Say no. "Yes," slips out.

He pulls himself up to sitting, leaning against his pile of pillows. "Sabrina Christy and I were classmates at the school I attended before Lincoln. We'd both been at a party a mutual friend held and we were drunk. I fooled around with one other person before but never had sex until that night. The condom my dad made me keep in my wallet busted when I tried putting it on, she accidently elbowed me in the face when she tried climbing on top of me in the back seat, and the whole thing was rushed.

"Honestly? I didn't really care at the time because all I could think about was that I was finally having sex. Her car was parked outside of the party so we both figured why not? Thankfully, she had a condom in her purse, but we were sloppy about the whole thing. It was awkward, Little Bird. I don't want that sort of experience with you."

My frown deepens. "You don't?"

He cups my cheek. "I want it to be *better*. You don't deserve some random backseat hookup. That shouldn't be your first time."

Heart racing, I try taking even breaths. "I just want to be good at it, but I don't know how. What if we decide this whole more-than-friends thing isn't for us?"

Both his brows raise. "Do you really think that'll happen?"

In truth, I don't. It's the gut feeling that tells me we're in for a ride. But I don't want to admit that because it seems weird to speak aloud. We're young. We have dreams beyond Lincoln. Nobody can be certain of what will happen weeks, months, or even a year from now.

"You're leaving soon," I tell him instead.

He pulls me down so our faces are close, his eyes piercing mine and jumpstarting my heart in a way nobody else has. "I'm coming back for you, Kinley. Trust me. When you're done with high school, it's us against the world."

My heart pounds so hard it hurts when he nuzzles his nose against mine. Breath against my lips, it's me who closes the distance between us to seal the feeling imbedded deep inside my chest. The first peck is quick, quicker than the one on Christmas Eve. I close my eyes and try not to think about anything other than him, than us, and his promise.

It's him who returns the kiss and holds the back of my head to him. His lips become firmer, rougher, as they work to part mine. Yet there's a softness to his movements—how he threads his fingers in my hair, how he holds me to him as his tongue touches mine. It sends jolts down my body until my palms find his chest and grip the t-shirt he's wearing. Trying my best to mimic what he does, our tongues twist and taste and tangle until I pull back out of breath.

His breath still dances on my lips, his nose brushing my cheek. I rest my forehead on his and squeeze the handful of cotton I hold. His hands drop to my hips, resting without any pressure or expectation for me.

And that's why I trust him—believe him.

"You promise?" I whisper, swallowing and letting my chest slowly rise through every bated exhale.

His fingers rub small circles over denim-clad hips. Not making another move to kiss me, he pulls me down until we're resting side by side. One of his arms drapes around my shoulders, keeping me locked in tight. My cheek rests against his pec, my palm just above his belly button.

He says, "Promise."

sixteen

Corbin / Present

My hands slowly map out soft curves until my fingers meet the scratchy denim hugging a slim waist. Subconsciously, I know it's all wrong. My fingertips should be teasing the worn elastic band of black leggings, fumbling to work past the onset of giggles from the slightest area where she's ticklish.

"Ryker." Her ass arches back and grinds into my front, causing my lips to nip the hollow of her neck that she exposes to me. "Not here."

"Not here," I repeat, popping the button and stalling

on the zipper. "You say that every time we meet, Beck. We can't get caught anymore. What are you afraid of?"

Her grip on the railing tightens, and I know the effects they'll use to emphasize the clear night will make the scene better. Our sins are masked in darkness, but our indiscretions are highlighted by the apartment behind us that my character never should have walked into.

The breathy sound of her voice says, "Us. That's what I'm afraid of. We aren't simple people. We ruin everything. We're bad."

My lips trail down the back of her neck, causing her breath to catch. "Nothing about us has ever been simple. That's why we work. We're complicated. Our love is complicated. Our situation—"

She turns and shoves my shoulders, but her effort is tactless. "Our *situation*, Ryker? I was engaged to some-body that I thought I could love. Ian is kind, and loyal, and everything I'm not. Wearing the ring he gave me reminded me of what kind of person I am—what we are. *Our* situation is ugly and messy and destroying me."

Ian's name is meant to induce anger, the kind that bulges my veins and reddens my face. I channel every-thing I have in personal experience to feel what it'd be like for Ryker to witness the woman he loves more than life itself settle for someone because she doesn't think she deserves happiness.

"You'll never love him the same way."

"Ryker, stop." She closes her eyes.

"You're guilting yourself."

"Ry—"

"You love *me*, Beck. Me." I slam my palm into my chest and step forward. "Our love is the truest kind because it's so ugly. Nobody gets a happy ending easily. Ian isn't meant for you. I am. He knows it. You know it. I know it."

A single tear streams down her face, but she's too stubborn to let me wipe it away. Instead, she steps back, reaching behind her and holding onto the cold railing that separates her from the night.

I see the pain shredding her up little by little, and my comfort would do nothing to hold the pieces together. She's self-destructing because she once told me she didn't love me before moving on to men who she tried her best to feel even the slightest bit of passion for.

"You're torturing yourself," I whisper, shaking my head and refraining from touching her damp cheeks. "You don't have to anymore. I forgive you. I..." My eyes trail over to where Kinley watches the scene unravel. "I love you even if I shouldn't, even when I remember every ounce of pain that our past brought us."

Buchannan throws his hands up. "Cut! What the hell was that, Callum? You're not supposed to look over here. I don't give a shit if you love me. You're supposed to deliver those lines to her—to Beck." He curses and gets off his chair, shaking his head and walking over to one of the camera guys.

My eyes stay unblinking on Kinley, whose lips are parted as she stares back. Her hands are molded together on her lap, flexing, like she wants to say or do something but holds herself back.

I mouth, *I remember.*

Her eyes close for a moment before she slides off her chair ... and walks away.

Something smacks my shoulder. "Dude, I was really feeling that scene and you had to go all method on us. What the fuck?"

Tipping my head back, I palm my eyes before stepping away from her. "I don't know, Liv. I just haven't been feeling myself lately."

"Why? Is it Lena?"

"No."

We walk over to where a couple chairs rest unoccupied and sit down. She doesn't bother rebuttoning her jeans, just leaves them undone while still sporting a see-through belly shirt that shows off her toned stomach and black bra underneath.

"Is it about Kinley?"

My head snaps in her direction. "What did you just say?"

She rolls her eyes and combs her fingers through her blonde tresses. "There are a lot of stupid people here, Callum. I'm not one of them. She's the only one who calls you Corbin. Usually you correct people or disengage. You let her though."

Trying to play it off, I say, "So?"

She eyes me. "Did you miss the part where I stated that I'm not stupid? You two stare at each other all the time. It's not like she's starstruck either. In fact, I think she hates your guts which is kind of amazing." She smiles when I flip her off. "That also probably means that you two know each other, and since Google is the world's best friend, one little search could tell me if there's a connection between the two of you."

On high alert, I straighten in my seat. "I really don't think —"

"You can hire people to delete your past, but the internet always has something." Her nose scrunches a little, then she shrugs. "Lincoln, huh? I never pictured you in a place so ... rural. Most of the pictures you get when you search the town are of cows."

"Jesus." My knee bounces with nerves until Olivia steadies it with her hand.

"Relax, *Corbin*. I'm not going to say anything to anybody." Her head tilts. "Why did you try so hard getting rid of your ties there? The newspaper picture of you in the school play was all it took to do a few more searches until I got the bigger picture."

"Does it matter?"

Liv rolls her eyes. "Just answer me this. What was she like back then?"

I want to look behind us where Kinley's chair is, but I know she won't be there. Blowing out a breath, I answer truthfully. "She hasn't changed at all."

Liv's eyes brighten. "It's pretty amazing if you think about it. Two well-known public figures came from the same small town."

"I moved there my senior year," I admit, studying the people setting the space back up where it was before I decided to stray from the script. Absentmindedly, I add, "Kinley became my best friend."

"No shit," Olivia breathes, sitting back in her chair and taking it in. "Guess that explains the familiarity between you. Wait—"

I look at her warily as a grin spreads across her face. Knowing what's coming, I close my eyes and pretend I'm anywhere else. What happened between Kinley and I shouldn't be discussed with co-workers.

Her expression is too giddy when I finally meet her eyes again. "Was she talking about you when we asked about the sex scene? I really want you to tell me yes."

Deadpan, I just stare at her.

She claps once. "Holy shit. She's seriously my hero. You don't even have to tell me. I can see it in your eyes. No man's ego could walk away unbruised from that brutal conversation. No wonder you came to the mystery man's defense so quickly. Was it like a virgin pact?"

Clicking my tongue, I stare at one of the assistants

repositioning the chair we'd accidentally knocked down in the process of our scene.

"No. It's none of your business."

Her hand clenches my wrist. "It's so my business. I already know the famous Corbin Callum took my favorite author's virginity, but you won't tell me who took yours?"

I just glare at her.

She groans. "Eliot Sanchez."

Why the hell is she bringing up a famous director's kid? "What about him?"

Her wink is playful. "He's who claimed my V-card. Right on set of his dad's feature film. There was a couch that—"

"Stop." I make a face. "I really don't want to know. Why are you even telling me?"

"So you'll tell me who took yours. Spill."

"Again … no."

"You're no fun!"

"You're nosey," I fire back.

"I'm mind blown," she corrects. "The chances of this sort of thing happening have to be pretty low. Like winning the lottery low. Or, I don't know, being attacked by a shark in a tornado low."

I stare at her. "Did you just make a *Sharknado* reference? Who even are you?"

Her scoff is nonthreatening. "A fan of unique storylines, that's who. But that is beside the point and you know it."

"Why do you want to know so bad?"

Lifting her shoulders, she crosses her legs and drapes an arm across the back of her seat. "I don't know. I'm a hopeless romantic who believes that things happen for a reason."

"And knowing who I lost my virginity to somehow helps you hold that belief?"

She smacks my arm. "The point I'm slowly putting together in my head is that you two seem to have gone through a lot but look where you are. You're both adults, both successful, and somehow found your way back to each other despite being in two totally different career paths. That means something."

Does it though? I want to believe the same thing, but there isn't anything we can do about it. Not publicly. I did my best at keeping Kinley out of the press when I started getting more attention, which was the only reason I got someone to take down anything they could about my past. Kinley always hated publicity and being the center of attention. I knew the second I opened up about my time in Lincoln, and the people in it, people would do anything to get a quick scoop on me.

Whether Kinley wants to believe it or not, I've always looked out for her. Even when she didn't realize it. Definitely when she didn't want me to.

"I'm not the only one she's slept with," I murmur begrudgingly, eye twitching from the fact I know all too goddam well.

Olivia doesn't have to ask to know that I'm still pissed off even after all these years. Was I a saint after I left town? No. But that didn't start until after I heard what she did. That's really when the tale of Kinley and Corbin became ugly.

Liv nudges my leg with her foot. "All due respect but I would hope not. Did you expect her to wait for you? That's what happened right? Small town love gone wrong?"

I don't answer.

"Do you mind me asking why you're still upset over something like that? It had to have happened a long time ago."

This time, my eyes do go over my shoulder at the spot Kinley stands. Her back is turned to me while she talks to Buchannan. His hand is on her arm and he's giving her a sleezy smile that makes me want to shove him away.

"It's not about when it happened," I tell her quietly. "It's about who it happened with."

Olivia waits for me to speak the memory I haven't thought of since I found out about it. That little nugget of information was one her brother fed me when I got back to town, driving the final nail in the coffin.

Too bad for you, you're too late.

My fist tightens and loosens.

She's with Zach.

"Whatever." I brush it off, standing up and nodding toward the markers on the floor. "I think we'll start reshooting in a few. Coming?"

Her eyes narrow. "You're seriously no fun when it comes to real life conversations."

I manage to chuckle. "Get your pleasure from someone else's pain. I can't keep getting you off with my misery alone."

"Misery, huh?" Her eyebrows wiggle. "It must be some strong feelings keeping you stuck in the past if that's how you feel about it."

"Shove it."

"Mm." She winks. "Maybe later, baby."

Rolling my eyes, we get back to our places just as Buchannan calls for the set to quiet down. After telling me not to mess up this take, he gestures to start rolling.

Kinley doesn't look at me.

I don't look at her.

I'm SURPRISED to see Kinley standing outside the door to my trailer when they call it for the day. After my screw up, I made sure to stay on track. Somehow, we got ahead and opted not to start filming tomorrow's scenes.

Slowing my steps when I see the lack of emotion on

her face, I mentally prepare myself for anything. I used to be able to read Kinley easily. Whatever she feels usually lingers in her eyes, lifts or lowers her lips, or causes the tiniest shift in her fair complexion.

Opening the door, I nod toward the inside. Contemplation washes over her features, and the dark tone of her brown hues make them look fear ridden. Blowing out a deep breath, I walk in without looking to see if she follows.

I kept my distance all day. Instead of seeking her out when she was alone, I made sure to keep busy that way I wasn't tempted to ask if she was all right after what happened the other day. She didn't show up the day after we slept together, telling someone she was on a strict deadline she needed to focus on.

Olivia took pity on me and we ate lunch together without her asking anymore questions about my past. It doesn't stop me from remembering different pieces of it —the good, bad, and everything in between. I've thought of countless ways I could have fixed what happened before realizing that I can't.

Grabbing a cold bottle of water from the fridge, I guzzle half of it before Kinley finally walks up the steps. She stands by the door, hesitant, watching me with blankness masking her features again.

I always loved knowing if she was happy, sad, excited, or angry. Half the time, the emotions were because of me. If I said or did something dumb, her nose would scrunch. If we set a date to watch a movie at one of our parents' houses, her eyes would brighten.

"What's wrong with you?" she says quietly, crossing her arms over her chest. The way her palms squeeze her opposite arms makes it look like she's hugging herself.

I lean against the counter where the fridge rests. "How long do you have?"

She doesn't respond.

Shrugging, I push myself up and walk over to the couch. I had no intention of staying late, but there's obviously something Kinley has to get off her chest.

In the matter of seconds, she lets it go. "I don't have very long left here, Corbin. While I'm still not keen on the casting choices for certain parts, I do want to make the most of the experience. Whatever stunt that was—"

"It wasn't a stunt," I cut her off calmly.

She blinks, her arms going to her sides for a moment before they start moving. "What the hell does that mean? That's one of the lines right from the book. It's not delivered that way. Beck needs to know that Ryker loves her even when she doesn't love herself. How can she understand that if he won't even look at her?"

Laughing is not what the situation calls for, and it gets me a hasty glare. "You're something else, Little Bird."

"Don't you *dare* call me that right now."

I scooch forward on the couch until I'm on the edge of the cushion. "It's your nickname, so I'm calling you it.

What happened between us doesn't change that. What kind of denial are you in? You said it yourself, that line is from the novel *you* wrote. Tell me what that says."

She pauses, her lips parting and closing for a moment before she finds her words. "It doesn't say anything. They're just — "

"You're lying."

"Would you quit cutting me off!" she yells, moving further into the trailer. "You don't get to dominate this conversation. You're reading into the script if you think I meant anything by that scene."

Head cocking, I set my water on the table in front of me. "What I don't understand is why Beck still pushes Ryker away when they finally have a chance to be together."

"You want to talk about the characters?"

I nod, sitting back again and throwing my arm over the back of the couch. "You wrote a strong, sexy, bold female who acts like she owns the world. Then you turn her into a completely different person when she's around Ryker."

Kinley wets her lips. "That's the point, Corbin. We're not ourselves around the people we care about because we're so focused on being exactly what that other person needs. Beck and Ryker could have given it a shot when they were younger, but Beck knew it wasn't what she needed. How many relationships last outside of high school?"

I don't have an answer, so I remain silent.

"Look," she says, taking a deep breath. "I don't expect you to understand Beck's character. Even after ... you know, what you told me about you and Lena. What matters is that Olivia gets it and plays her perfectly. Beck's guilt for seeing Ryker struggle through relationships and their own friendship over the years made her feel like she was the enemy. If her best friend couldn't be happy, why should she? That kind of things holds onto a person."

Eyes narrowing, I say, "You made her feel like the antagonist in her own story. Why?"

At first, I don't think she'll answer. Her eyes go down to the carpeted floor, to the walls that have a few landscape paintings on them, to the rack of clothes for my character in the corner. She takes in the room before she can look me in the eye again, and when she does, there's something broken in the depths staring back.

"Sometimes we can't help but feel like the bad guy in our lives." Her fingers trail along the molding that separates the wood paneling and beige wallpaper covering the wall. "Like maybe if we did something different it'd change the outcome. Or like ... if *we* were different then we'd be happier somehow."

She blames herself for what happened?

"Fuck," I breathe, standing up and walking over to her. She tenses when I tilt her chin up to meet my eyes. "You're not the bad guy, Little Bird. I made a promise to you that I didn't keep because I'm a selfish bastard. There is nothing you need to change about yourself."

Her eyes may be locked with mine, but they're so full of disbelief that they're distant. "You say that now, but those were the words I needed to hear when I was seventeen and thinking there was something wrong with me. Was I not skinny enough? Pretty enough? Did I stop believing in you the way you believed in me? Was there somebody else? I kept wondering if it was because I was in school still, or focused on my writing, or just not good enough..."

It's hard to swallow past the emotion lodged in my throat. "That was never the case, and I wish I could go back again and make you never think that was why."

"Again?" she repeats. "What...?"

Clearly her brother never mentioned our little meetup at the store even when I told her to ask him about it. "It doesn't matter now. You were right to call me out on being a dickhead about, well, everything. I never wanted to be in Lincoln to begin with and was so determined to get out of there that I didn't think about anybody else. That wasn't about you."

She tries stepping back, but I don't let her. My hand wraps around her arm, not holding too tightly but enough where she can't pull away. I can feel her warmth, smell the faintest hint of sweet peach like the lotion she used to love so much, and get taken back to the last time we stood this close.

We looked at each other differently.

With love. Hope. Faith that it'd work out.

"I fucked up," I whisper. "That's on me."

"Corbin…" Her voice cracks. "I refuse to put myself in this situation again. I didn't come here to rehash what happened the other night. I came to tell you not to do what you did today. If people find out about us … everything changes."

My other hand moves to her face, caressing her soft cheek and smiling when I realize there's not a stitch of makeup covering her skin.

Her breath catches and I feel it ricochet off the heel of my palm. In my chest is the quickening pace of a heartbeat that hasn't moved so desperately in a long time. Not since a girl with the strangest colored hair showed me the school, became my friend, and then my biggest regret.

Not one audition has allowed me to feel the anticipation that having her in my hold has given me in mere seconds. Warm flesh, hot breath, thick emotion.

"I'm sorry," I whisper, before bending down and brushing my lips over hers. It's the softest touch, the sweetest torture, and before I can deepen it like my hardening cock wants to, I'm being shoved away and slapped with a force that leaves my cheek stinging and my vision doubled before regaining reality.

Tears spill down Kinley's cheeks when I finally blink away the shock of what just happened, and everything I felt from her nearness melts into the heaviest guilt.

But nothing matches the feelings that cement in my chest when she opens her mouth and spits out, "I *hate* you for making me like this. Weak. Angry. Second best. Like I somehow deserve this."

Red face to match her bloodshot eyes, she backs away and touches her lips before choking out a sob that has me frozen to my spot.

"It doesn't matter that you and your wife decided not to work it out, Corbin. The world thinks you're some happy couple. People on this lot think we're strangers who met to put something heartbreakingly beautiful on the big screen. We're fooling everyone and torturing ourselves with what-if."

"It doesn't have to be—"

"Yes, it does!" She clenches her hands into fists by her sides and blows out a deep breath while staring at me. "Who are you trying to kid? Do you really think we can go back to pretending like we can attend each other's formal events together like nobody would question it? Men and women can't be friends in your industry without everyone picking them apart. You may be used to that lifestyle, but I'm not. And you damn well know that we're not just friends. Once upon a time we were, but we'll never get that back."

I step toward her, running my palms down my thighs. "If that's what you want, we can make it work.

We promised each other the Oscars and RITA Awards, remember? I do. You'd wear a long black dress with a slit up the leg and matching flats because heels make you too unsteady. I'd wear a black tuxedo and a silver tie because it matches my eyes and we'd have a great time. We can be those people again."

"I don't want to be," she whispers. She shakes her head and backs closer to the door. "I don't want to remember what it was like to have my hopes up just to get hurt so badly."

"It won't … it'll be different."

"You're right." She looks down. "It'll be so much worse next time. You want to know why Beck chose Ian? Why she let him put a ring on her finger instead of Ryker? It's simple. We settle because we're afraid the love that's meant for us will destroy us completely."

This time, I have nothing to offer her. No words, no gestures, no argument that says differently. She told me once that she loved how authors' minds worked because they told a truth that nobody wants to hear. Life, love, everything can shatter you in an instant, but writers find a way to make it sound like the perfect way to go.

When she all but bolts out of my trailer, I realize one thing is for certain. If nothing had changed before, everything has now. Any shred of hope to rekindle a friendship with the girl I once considered the only special person in my life, is long gone.

seventeen

KINLEY / Present

MY TIRED EYES burn the longer I go through the notes littering my manuscript in front of me. The red ink is everywhere, circling words, and crossing out sentences. The slightest tension in the back of my neck has me dropping my pen onto the bed and massaging the base of my skull.

Sliding off the mattress, I go to my purse and dig through it until the bottle I'm looking for is in my hand. When I see it's empty, I groan and look at the time on the alarm clock by the bed.

Considering where I am, there's no doubt I could

find a store to buy medicine this time of night. Anything to ease the pain quickly forming in my temples.

Trying to Google places in walking distance has me more confused than anything, so I slip into the clothes I wore today and walk downstairs to the front desk.

The older gentleman working the night shift looks up from the computer and smiles at me. "Ms. Thomas. How can I help you?"

I grip my purse and note his nametag. "Is there a drugstore nearby that sells Motrin, Matt? Or a convenience store I can walk to?"

He hesitates before standing straighter. "I would suggest not walking anywhere this time of night on your own. However, I can call a car or even get someone to fetch the medication for you."

I blink. What? "No, that's okay. I can get it myself. If you can just give me an address or tell me how to get there…"

He nods once and clicks a few times on the computer before jotting an address down on hotel stationary. "If I may, there is another option to get there that's safer."

Before he can say what it is, someone calls my name. The man behind the desk nods once with a faint smile on his face as he turns back to whatever he was working on before I came down.

"What are you doing here?" My greeting isn't

friendly, but it could be ruder given our present company.

Corbin stuffs his hands in his pockets. "I was trying to gather the courage to talk to you. To be honest, I was just getting ready to leave."

"Good," slips out before I can stop it.

I begin walking toward the double doors, tightening the jacket around me now that the mid-summer sun has set. Not so surprisingly, Corbin follows close behind me until we stop outside the hotel.

"You can't just go out on your own."

I turn. "Excuse me?"

He sighs. "Don't be like that. You know it isn't smart to walk around by yourself in a city like this. Plus, you don't know where you're going, do you?"

"And you do?"

"I've lived around here longer."

Like I don't know that. I scoff and start walking in a random direction, noting the semi-crowded sidewalk. People ignore me for the most part, some give me a weird look, and others bump into me without caring.

A hand grabs my wrist, which I'm about to shove away when Corbin's scratchy voice breaks through my caution. "Stop, Little Bird."

I whip my arm away.

He jabs behind him. "My car is parked over there. Just let me take you where you need to go, okay? It'll be painless."

"To you," I mutter.

For some reason, he chuckles. "Yeah, maybe. Still, I'm not letting you wander around on your own. It's supposed to rain too."

My eyes go up to the slightly cloudy sky. Not wanting to take a risk, I reluctantly follow him back to the hotel. He says something to the doorman and slaps his arm with a smile before pulling out his keys and guiding me to a sleek back car parked off to the side.

"Looks expensive," I note as he opens the passenger door for me. Sliding in, I examine the inside dash that's covered in screens and buttons that I'm afraid to touch. He closes the door and jogs around the front.

My fingers run across the black plastic in front of me and drag down to the glove compartment. Unlatching it while he starts the car and turns out onto the street, I dig through the random papers, napkins, and sunglasses before making a face.

"Looking for something?" he muses.

The truth just sort of comes out. "I thought there'd be something interesting in here. I don't know. Condoms, a thousand dollars, something."

His laugh has me eying him. "You think I'd just keep a thousand dollars in my car for anyone to steal?"

I don't answer.

"What's in your glove compartment?" he questions, slowing as we hit lines of traffic.

I think about it, not really knowing a solid answer.

I'm pretty sure the only thing in mine is the car insurance papers and maybe chapstick that's long since melted. Once upon a time, I kept a familiar burgundy notebook in there to read through or write in if I had an idea when I was out. Now it's in a box in my office closet with the other notebooks I've filled with story outlines and one-liners that I've used along the years. I refuse to take it out and trace the gold lettering I've spent a lot of time staring at since Corbin gave it to me for our first and only Christmas.

"Nothing important, I guess," he concludes when I say nothing.

For some reason, I smile at the memory of the vehicle I rode around in with him. "You used to have such random stuff in your Jeep. The cup holders had coins filling them so our drinks never fit right, your glove compartment had fast food menus and napkins, and the little console on the side held your thirty million sunglasses."

He grins at me. "You always judged me for how many shades I had. I never teased you about your shoe collection. Or the ridiculous amount of pillows you always kept on your tiny ass bed. How did you even fit?"

Gavin would get annoyed with me about that too. It was rare as we got older that he'd hang out with me in my room, but sometimes we'd put on Netflix on my laptop and junk out. It never stopped him from buying me new pillows if he found ones that reminded him of me.

"I miss that Jeep," he tells me, looking into the side-view before moving to a different lane. "I considered getting a new one but didn't think it'd work well for what I need here."

Looking at the screen in the middle of the dash, I note all the different options. "Seems like you can do way more with this thing."

"It works."

I roll my eyes. "My car doesn't even have heated seats. You should be more grateful for what you have."

He's quiet for a moment. "You're right."

After a few more minutes, we slow down near a lit-up drugstore. He pulls into the parking lot and shuts off the car. His body turns to mine as he grabs something from the back.

"Ready?" Pulling a baseball cap onto his head to cover his dark hair, he smiles.

"You need a fake mustache too?"

He rolls his eyes and pulls sunglasses from a little compartment above the rearview mirror that I didn't see before. "You joke, but you'll see why it's important."

"You're kidding right?"

The shades cover his eyes. "Nope."

Opening his door, he nods his head. "Are you coming? You need some Motrin, don't you? I could grab a few things too while we're out."

My hand stalls on the lever of the door, watching him warily. "Why are you doing this? Trying so hard?"

His response is instant. "Because you deserve it."

I swallow and open the door, absentmindedly following him inside. His palm lightly rests on the small of my back as we walk to the aisle we need.

There are only a few people in the store, which doesn't surprise me since it's going on midnight. According to the sign in the glass door, they're open twenty-four-seven. I suppose given the demographic, it's probably a good thing.

Corbin picks up a bottle and shakes it. "Is this going to work, or do you need a bigger one?"

"That'll work."

He keeps hold of it and continues walking down the aisle until his eyes scan the new one he wants. When I notice the candy along the shelves, I roll my eyes.

"Isn't it a bit late for candy?"

His gasp is amusing and overdone. "I seem to recall a girl who informed me that there's never a bad time for candy."

Pretty sure the time he's referring to is the same night I ate way too much sugar and puked my guts out. Corbin had to hold my hair back and find a store that was still open to get me ginger ale and anti-nausea medicine so my stomach would settle.

"Pick your poison." He already has our normal in

his hand, but my eye goes to the peanut butter cups that's in front of me.

"I'm paying for my own stuff."

"Mmhmm."

I eye him. "Don't be stupid."

He just winks.

We walk further down the aisle. "So, you don't have things to do other than lurk outside my hotel building in the middle of the night? Seems awfully similar to a guy I used to know that creeped outside of restaurants after dark."

"Weird coincidence," he remarks. "I normally go to bed after I get home, but we have the weekend off. Gives me time to get out."

"And lurk?"

He eyes me. "I like to think of it as helping people in need."

Wow. "So charitable these days."

As we enter another aisle, a younger woman who's carrying a red basket stops in the middle and stares in our direction. Corbin reaches for something in the clearance section without noticing, but I can't help but watch the blonde woman's lips part. He takes his glasses off and squints at the device hanging on the rack.

"Uh…" I tap Corbin's shoulder.

He looks at me with his brows raised. I subtly gesture my head in the other direction and watch him turn to see what I'm trying to tell him. I think he curses softly under his breath.

"You're Corbin Callum, right?" the woman says, still gawking.

I lean in and whisper, "Should have invested in a mustache."

His shoulder bumps mine. "Hello," he tells the woman with a charming smile.

I think she says something, but I can't be sure. Her lips do a weird fish thing like she's trying to gather her words. I try not to giggle, but it slips through.

Corbin walks over with a swagger to his strut that has me rolling my eyes. His sunglasses get clipped on the collar of his shirt before he reaches his free hand out to shake hers. For a few seconds, she just stares at it like she can't believe someone like him is willing to touch her.

"What's your name, sweetheart?"

Oh, for the love of —

The woman finally collects herself before taking his hand and holding onto it with both of hers. I nibble my lip to suppress my smile as they talk in low murmurs, trying to play it off and look through the odd and end items for sale. From the corner of my eye, I notice a few other people with cell phones gather on the other end of the aisle.

Nerves picking up, I try getting Corbin's attention as he speaks to his fan. The others point their phones in his direction and murmur to each other. I grip the candy in my hand and keep my head down.

"Corbin," I whisper as I walk casually closer to him. Pretending to browse the coffee mugs near me, I clear my throat. "Corbin. There is a crowd starting."

He looks from the woman across the aisle and nods once with pressed lips. "It was nice meeting you, but I need to go."

I take the opportunity to walk past them and toward the register. My headache is becoming worse by the second and I'm half tempted to just leave without worrying about the stuff we grabbed.

Corbin appears next to me and drops his items on the counter with mine and pulls out a few twenty-dollar bills. He drops it on the counter and asks the man working to bag quickly and keep the change.

I don't try to argue with him about paying as he slides his glasses back on and accepts the bags before I can even reach for them.

His hand goes back to the small of my back as we walk toward the door. People call out his name and ask him to sign something for them, causing us both to pick up speed. My heart races so fast it hurts, and there's a rush throughout my limbs that has me overheating in my jacket.

Once we're inside the car, he makes quick to start it and back out of the space. "Are you okay?"

All I can do is stare out the windshield as he pulls

into the crowded street. Someone honks and passes us, but not before holding up their middle finger in our direction. I lean back and grip the armrest next to me, trying to even my breathing.

"Breathe, Little Bird," he directs softly.

I close my eyes and nod.

"You're pale."

"I don't feel well."

He curses and the bag rustles next to me. The bottle of tablets shakes and appears in my line of vision. My hand shakily reaches out and accepts them, struggling with the cap.

"Hey," he comforts, slowing down at a red light. He takes the bottle and opens it. "I know this is rough, but we're okay. There's a water bottle right here, drink some and take the medicine. You'll feel better in a bit."

My eyes go to the half-empty plastic bottle he's referring to between us. I must have made a face as he chuckled and passed it to me.

"Don't look so disgusted." Wrapping my fingers around the bottle, I glance up at him. His eyes are focused in front of him, waiting for the light to change. "It isn't like we haven't exchanged bodily fluids before."

My voice is hoarse. "Don't remind me."

His lips kick up on the corners.

After I swallow the pills, I hold the water bottle in my lap and stare down at my hands. The pad of my thumb runs down the ribbed sides, and I watch as little water droplets slide down the inside of the plastic.

"Thank you," I find myself whispering.

His hand reaches over and takes mine. "I know you don't want to hear this, but I'm here for you."

Without thinking, I flip my hand over so our palms cup each other's. He squeezes my hand, and I squeeze my eyes closed. The heat from his touch eases the panic in my chest, but it doesn't lessen the other feeling swarming my stomach.

The flutters.

The warning signs.

The alarms.

Our drive is silent.

eighteen

KINLEY / 16

THE FOGGINESS of being freshly woken by someone shaking my shoulder has my eyes peeling open to be met by silver ones. Body locking, I sit up and let the blanket wrapped around me fall into a bundle on my lap.

Thankfully, I'm sporting my decent pajamas instead of the ratty tee I originally had on before bed. I guess spilling hot chocolate over me had its perks.

"What are you doing here?" I whisper, rubbing my eyes and staring at the time on my clock. It's not even one in the morning.

"I got it, Little Bird."

I blink slowly, too tired to follow.

He sits down on the bed. "I got the role in the movie. *Better*. They're going to give me a part that gets more screen time."

My eyes widen and I'm suddenly awake as I launch myself at him in a tight hug. "Corbin! That is so amazing, congratulations. How did you find out? Did they call? Email? Facebook message? Morse code?"

"Morse —" He shakes his head and chuckles quietly, pulling away. "You're nuts. No, Daniel called me about half an hour ago. He's friends with one of the casting crew and wanted to tell me himself."

I bounce on the bed and smile so big it physically hurts. "You're going to be in a movie. A *movie*. Corbin Callum — actor." My arms pebble with goosebumps. "People will want pictures and autographs and get all weird and giggly when they're near you."

"Whoa." His smile is full of amusement as he shoves me over so he can sit beside me. "I wouldn't get too ahead of ourselves. This is only a made for television movie, remember?"

I swat the back of my hand against his chest and lean into him, collecting the blanket and offering him some. He accepts and maneuvers under the covers, kicking his shoes off in the process.

"Lots of people watch those movies," I tell him, my cheek resting on his shoulder. "Plus, it shouldn't matter if it's *just* made for TV. You're still in a movie, on a screen, where anyone can watch. It's insane."

His lips find the top of my head, causing me to close my eyes and curl into him. "I was starting to think my dad was right."

I straighten up and stare at him until he meets my eyes. "Don't doubt yourself. I've watched you practice your lines so many times, Corbin. You're amazing. A natural. This isn't going to be the only part you get."

He studies me for a second with those intense eyes before smiling. "You're my biggest cheerleader, you know that?"

I playfully jab his ribs. "I'm your biggest fan, too. Tell all the screaming women that when you encounter them."

"I'll make a shirt," he says seriously.

We sit like that for a moment, just watching each other in the tight proximity of my twin bed. The white down comforter has hair from our dog napping on it when I'm writing, and the many pillows I own are scattered on the floor instead of perched on the bed that way I have room to sleep. There's a gray throw blanket that my Grandma gave me for my birthday last year that's hanging off the edge of the mattress from my usual restlessness.

Resting back again, I give him a nudge with my shoulder. "You should really thank your parents. You've got the looks *and* the name. I have no doubt in my mind that you're going to be everywhere. Then I can brag about you to everyone I know."

"What about you, huh?"

"What about me?"

"You're going to have books with your name out there for everyone to fangirl." His hand finds mine over the blankets, our fingers playing tug-of-war.

"One day."

"It'll happen, Little Bird."

"Mm."

Sleepiness washes over me again.

"Kinley?"

I look up at him. "Yeah?"

His eyes dip down to my lips. "Thank you for being there for me. It means more than you know, especially with Dad…"

I wet my bottom lip. "You know I've got your back, superstar. And like I said before, your dad loves you. He's just struggling."

"And you?"

I blink. "You really have to ask?"

Instead of smiling, he leans in and bumps his nose with mine. His warm breath invites me to tilt my chin up and capture his lips the same time he brushes mine. One of his hands cradles my face as I sit there and absorb the minty taste of his breath. Collecting enough courage, I make a move to straddle his lap, forcing him to shift to the center of the bed so I have room. My knees rest on either side of him, his hands grasping my cotton-clad hips.

"Hey," he whispers, squeezing me. "I'm not sure what you're thinking right now. Talk to me, Little Bird."

I let out a shaky breath. "I'm thinking that I'm happy for you. I'm excited you get to start living your dream. And I'm thinking … that I'm not thinking at all."

My lips go to one cheek, then the other. Slowly, I trail them over his lips and leave a barely-there kiss like the first one he ever gave me. His fingertips twitch on my hips but stay where they are. Letting me explore, I wiggle on his lap until he bites back a groan. My spine straightens when I feel him harden beneath me. Our eyes meet and his cheeks pinken like mine.

"Corbin?"

I think his throat bobs. "Yeah?"

"Do you think … I mean, would it be okay if we, uh…" I lick my lips and feel my confidence wavering by the self-doubt increasing in the pit of my stomach.

His fingers find the hem of my shirt. "May I?" He tugs the material up, leaving my heart racing over what will happen if I say yes.

I nod in a daze, letting him peel the shirt off me and let it drop on the floor. His eyes widen as he takes in the sports bra I'm wearing. My boobs aren't very big — barely a B cup. But he looks at them like he's never seen something so beautiful, and my entire body blushes over the light in his eyes.

My hands go to his sweatshirt, the AC/DC one with the red lettering peeled and faded. He lifts his arms and lets me take it off him, revealing a thin sleeveless top underneath. I study his lean torso and how his breathing picks up. The bulge twitching under me grows harder the longer I stare.

Swallowing, I lift my gaze. "Show me what to do?" The question is soft, like a quiet demand as my pleading eyes stay unblinking on his.

He reaches behind him and takes off his shirt, tossing it on the floor with mine. My palms go to his bare skin, leaving goosebumps over my arms and shivers down his body as I explore. I know he sometimes runs, but he's cut like he works out too—not overly muscular, but lean. Strong. Beautiful.

His mouth finds mine as he holds me to him, my pelvis grinding down involuntarily. He bites down on my bottom lip and groans the same time I let out a soft gasp. Carefully, he trades positions. My back hits the mattress as he sits up and plays with the hem of my pajama pants. Without words, he questions me with a tip of his head and raised brow.

All I can do is nod and watch as he slides down the bottoms, revealing the cotton panties underneath. They're plain blue, lighter than my favorite color, and not very sexy. But he doesn't seem to care because he's focused on my body. I'm self-conscious as his eyes trail over me from top to bottom, and hyperaware that my stomach and thighs show my love of sugar and carbs.

But. He. Doesn't. Care.

"You're beautiful, Little Bird."

Oncoming emotion washes over me, leaving tears in my eyes. His appearance blurs, but I can see the worry in his features.

"Do you want to stop?" Withdrawing, he watches me carefully, unsure.

"No. I just…" I wipe my face as the tears leak down my cheeks. "I'm sorry. Nobody has ever called me that before and it's … nice. More than nice."

His smile graces his face. "It's the truth. You're beautiful and you're mine. Right, Kinley? You're mine?"

I swallow. "Yours."

It seems like the rest of our clothes disappear in a blur of fumbling hands and soft curses. He nearly trips when he takes off his jeans and stumbles when I help him get my bra off. We stare intensely at each other when we're completely exposed, and I have the need to cover my body with the comforter because of it.

He doesn't let me though. When he climbs on the bed, he kisses me softly, intently, with purpose. Murmuring compliments, making me blush, his fingers trail over my naked skin and make me squirm. Heat rises between my legs when his hands draw nearer to a place only mine has ever been.

"We can stop," he reminds me.

My hands grip his shoulders. "Do you think we're moving too fast? It's only been a few weeks since we even admitted we like each other. And we just talked about the whole inexperience thing and kissing and Sabrina Christy and—"

"You remember her name?" He chuckles.

"Yeah."

He shakes his head, kissing me again. "I don't think we know how to go slow, Little Bird. We're meant to soar. Fly. Do what we want. You and I defy all odds, don't you think?"

I take a deep breath and find myself nodding again, cupping his face and tracing his features as he watches me.

He captures my lips with his again and whispers, "Fly with me, Little Bird."

And I do.

The moment is slow and painful and awkward, but beautiful and emotional and consuming. He gives me pain and takes it away with sobering kisses and covers my soft noises and accepts my scraping nails.

Corbin Callum and I cement something that makes me feel like a different person. Happy. Loved. Cared for. Scared. Nervous. Excited. I give him something that I have no doubt I'll remember for life.

We fly. Soar just like he says.

When it's over, we both get dressed—me in his AC/DC sweatshirt and my pajamas, and him in his tank top and jeans.

For the longest moment, we just lay there in silence, catching our breaths and absorbing the moment. My chest tightens, and my core hurts, and my eyes prickle with the swelling emotion from what we've done.

"Corbin?"

"Hmm."

"How did you even get in here?"

"Climbed the tree by the hallway window," he murmurs sleepily.

I sit up slightly. "You did not!"

He looks over and grins at me. "Your family keeps the spare key on the top of the door jamb, Kinley. It's not hard to find."

Shaking my head, I smile to myself and move closer into his side. "You have a habit of stalking me, Corbin Callum."

"Why the full name?"

"You're not denying the stalker claims?"

"I only stalk the pretty ones."

"Wow." I laugh into his chest which I use as a pillow despite the others around us. "You should try getting cast as Ted Bundy in a Lifetime movie. You'd be perfect."

"Hardy har har."

After a moment, I say, "You were born with a name meant to be known by the world. I mean, hopefully not as a serial killer, but…"

"Go to sleep, Little Bird," he muses.

"Fine." I close my eyes. "But you need to leave before anyone realizes you're here, okay?"

I don't hear his response.

"ABSOLUTELY FUCKING NOT," a voice booms somewhere close by.

It doesn't take long to assess the overheated body pressed way too close to me before understanding what the unwanted wakeup call is for. When I crack my eyes open to see my brother fuming at my doorway I want nothing more than to hide under my blanket and pretend he can't see Corbin.

"Morning, Gavin."

He walks in and rips the blankets off, quickly covering his eyes with his hands. "You better both be wearing clothes. I don't want to kick a naked boy's ass."

Corbin jerks up, somehow head butting me in the process. I wince and rub my forehead before smacking Gavin. "We're not naked," I hiss, feeling the sting of heat encompassing my entire body.

Gavin looks at Corbin with narrow eyes before pulling him up by his shirt and shoving him toward the door. "I'm hiding the spare key and chopping down any trees that he might be able to climb. You're lucky Mom and Dad didn't find you two in here."

I quickly get up and yank on Gavin's sweatshirt to force him to stop pushing Corbin out of my room. There's discomfort between my legs that I push past, trying not to give myself away. "Stop! We didn't do anything. He came over to tell me some good news and we fell asleep."

Grabbing Corbin's shoes from the floor by my bed, I pass them to him. He stays silent as he kneels and slides them on, tightening the laces while Gavin and I stare each other down.

"Dad would kill him," he points out.

"Dad doesn't have to know."

His eyes narrow. "You can't have boys in your room, Kinley. You're like twelve. That's inappropriate."

My mouth gapes. He did *not* just call me twelve. I'm more mature than him in every way except age. He may have five years on me, but that's all he does.

"Rebecca Davenport."

His lips part.

"Stacy Smith."

His eyes narrow.

"You smoked weed with Tyler Bowen."

"How do you know all that?"

Crossing my arms on my chest in challenge, I meet his gaze firmly. "Because I'm not an idiot, but you are. Rebecca stumbled half-drunk into my room one night and got all giggly and apologetic when she thought it was the bathroom. Stacy told the entire school you and her were going steady after your little sleepover, and you smelled like skunk right after coming home from hanging out with Tyler and that other moron he's always with."

Gavin remains quiet.

Corbin stuffs his hands in the pockets of his jeans. "I should go. I'm sorry for falling asleep. We were really just talking."

Slowly, Gavin turns to face him. "I don't like you."

"Gavin!"

Corbin nods. "Duly noted."

"Ignore him," I tell Corbin.

Gavin shakes his head. "Good luck getting him out of here. Dad has been up for over an hour. Pretty sure he's on the computer."

Before he can walk out, I grab his arm. "I haven't said anything to them about your conquests. The least you can do is help me."

One of his dark eyebrows raises. "Can I speak to you ... *alone*?"

Corbin puts his hands up and walks toward the door. "I'll just ... be somewhere."

"You do that," Gavin grumbles, walking into my room and closing the door in Corbin's face before I can stop him.

I push his shoulder. "What is your problem? I don't

say anything to you about who you spend time with. I'm obviously trustworthy for not ratting you out about the stupid stuff you do to disrespect Mom and Dad. What's the big deal?"

He gestures toward the hall. "The big deal is that guy is going to hurt you, Kinley! I've told you once and I'll tell you again. He will leave. He's going to leave this town and he's going to leave you. You think I'm a moron, but something happened between you two. Don't start—" His warning gaze cuts me off from arguing. "I don't care if something happened last night or not. You look at him in a new way and it can only end badly. He's graduating in June. Then what?"

We haven't discussed what will happen when he graduates. Just that he promised to come back for me. He *promised*.

His voice becomes softer. "You want to know why I slept with random people and smoked weed and lost my shit for a while? Aimee."

I knew he took their breakup hard, but he never wanted to talk about it. He seemed fine for a while, focusing on work and building his farm up to make more money. I knew better than to bring her up because he'd shut down.

"First loves hurt, Kin. They suck." His hand raises to comb over his short hair. "The last thing I want for you is to get too invested in something that's inevitable."

"What if it's not?"

"Not what?"

"Inevitable?"

The look he gives me is full of doubt. "I always liked how you saw the best in people. Even when I was a total dick to you, you'd forgive me when I didn't deserve it. When Mom and Dad make comments that upset you about your writing, you brush it off and smile. There's only so much a person can take though. What if this is what breaks you?"

My frown deepens. "Way to have faith in me, big brother. Do you think I'm that weak?"

He sighs and rubs the back of his neck. "I think that being in love changes us. Take it from someone who knows. We get consumed so quickly in another person that we lose ourselves along the way. When you stop guarding yourself, everything is easier. Falling. Feeling. Hurting. I let what Aimee did to me ruin a lot of good shit in my life over the past couple of years."

"That doesn't mean I'll be the same."

"No," he agrees. "Knowing you, you'll be better than anything bad that can happen. I read the story you got published in that literary magazine. I don't doubt you'd channel everything you have in making something of yourself—with or without him."

He seems to emphasize the without him bit, making me close my eyes in frustration. I love Gavin even if his protective nature drives me nuts. I know people whose siblings don't care like he does, so I'm grateful. I just wish he'd let me make my own decisions without making me feel dumb for choosing to feel optimistic.

Instead of continuing the argument that'll get us nowhere, I relent, "Emotions are a good motivator for writing."

"Like heartbreak," he murmurs.

I glare. "Or love."

He just opens the door and shoots me a wary look over his shoulder. One that my gut tells me to consider. To believe.

I wish I had.

nineteen

CORBIN / Present

THE SOUND of my phone buzzing somewhere beside me has my hand absentmindedly whipping toward the offensive noise until I'm knocking shit over in the process. I groan loudly when it doesn't stop, sitting up and pressing the red button I see immediately in the corner.

Faceplanting back into the mattress, I'm half asleep when my phone starts making noise again. Cursing, I peel myself from the warm sheets and pick up the device. Tempted to throw it at the wall, my shoulders tense when I see the name displayed on the screen.

WHERE THE LITTLE BIRDS GO

Sighing, I accept the call. "Hi, Mom."

"Corbin," she says in her usual soft tone. She never changes her outlook on me, even when shit hits the fan in my life. "You're not still sleeping, are you? It's after ten in the morning."

Eyes widening a little at the news, I glance at the time displayed on the top of my screen to confirm she's right. I don't know the last time I slept this long. It was well past three in the morning before I got back home after dropping Kinley back off at the hotel and making sure she got to her room safely. The color on her face seemed to come back, giving me the tiniest comfort in letting her be for the night without too much guilt.

I scratch my nose and roll my shoulders back in a needed stretch. "Why are you calling, Mom? Don't get me wrong, it's good to hear from you. I figured I'd just check in later."

The pause doesn't prepare me for the quiet sigh I hear from her end. I never mean to come off like an asshole, but I don't have time to talk to her as much as she'd like. Occasionally we'll catch up for an hour or so before one of us has to go, and sometimes we'll make plans to meet up.

But never in Lincoln.

My mother has travelled to over twenty cities to see me depending on where I'm filming. I'll buy both her and Dad a ticket, not that he ever uses it, and fly them to me so we can catch up. I get us lunch, coffee, a souvenir, and ask how things are going in her life before zoning out when she tells me about Dad having problems. His problems aren't mine anymore.

"There are pictures of you and Kinley all over the news," is the last thing I expect her to say. The exhaustion latched onto me is long gone as I put the phone on speaker and quickly search the internet.

Kinley's face is grainy based on the cell phone pictures taken, but you can still tell who it is. She tries covering her face with her hair, but it doesn't mask it completely. And the picture of us walking out with me touching her on the back?

"Fuck."

"Corbin," Mom chides.

Rolling my eyes at the fact she still hates me cursing despite seeing almost all the movies I've been in that has me doing worse, I scroll through the various tabloid articles.

Most of them are innocent. Some mention the movie and speculate that our outing is purely to boost promotion. Others are nothing more than assumptions to get a rise out of people.

Corbin Callum seen out with new woman.

Author involved with movie star.

New Hollywood affair?

I scooch back until my bare back hits the bedframe behind me for support. "She had a headache that's all. I took her to get some medicine. People need to calm down."

"Why were you with her?"

Because I'm sick of not being.

"We're working together, Mom." I don't analyze the piss poor lie that I'm sure she doesn't believe for a second. I could always fool everyone but her growing up.

When she does speak, my chest tightens at the words she chooses carefully. "I'll always love her like a daughter. That girl is special, Corbin. She always has been, and she always will be. You need to leave her be."

My nostrils flare as I sit up straighter. "I haven't done anything—"

I can picture her shaking her graying head at me. "Sweetie, I will always love you and choose your side, but there are certain situations I will not support. I understand why you left to pursue your career, but you can't have it all."

"I don't want it all."

She simply hums in disbelief.

"I don't," I all but growl.

"Tell me. How is Lena doing?"

That silences me.

Lena and I texted a few times over the past couple of days but haven't called or Skyped once since Kinley walked back into my life. I know that she's busy with

B. CELESTE

her family and whoever else in Greece, and I'm trying
to scrape by with my sanity here.

The reality is, Lena and I are nothing more than two
people who should have never said I do. But we did.
We chose to pretend like what we felt was love—like it
was enough. I want to believe that I did love her … *do*
love her, but I also know that it's not the same love I've
always felt for Kinley.

There's a soft clicking. "You did the right thing by
letting Kinley live her life all these years, Corbin. Why
change her world again? She's been through enough."

My palm coasts down my face until it hits the scruff
lining my jaw. "Everyone goes through a breakup, Ma.
It's not the end of the world. We both know she's
stronger than that."

To my surprise, my mother scoffs. It's something
I've rarely heard her do. In fact, I could count the
amount of times she's done it on one hand. Most of
them involve my Dad saying stupid shit, which means
I'm about to get it.

"Have you even gotten to know her?"

"I know her already."

"You don't."

"Jesus, Mom. What does it matter? She still loves
reading, writing, sugar—"

"How has she spent the past few years?"

My lips part.

"Where does she live?"

I blink.

"What makes her who she is today?"

There's no answer I can offer her.

"You never used to be so selfish." Her words startle me. "There was always a reason to justify you taking classes and auditioning because you made time for other things. I don't know who you are anymore, Corbin. It scares me. It really does."

My throat bobs. "Mom…"

She speaks softly again. "I didn't call to upset you. Someone needs to talk you down from the high you're living before you take everyone down with you. Do you really want that for her?"

No.

"I didn't think so," she concludes.

"You love her too," I finally say.

"I'm not the only one."

Dad.

Her family.

Me.

I know who she's referring to.

"But that's a problem, baby boy."

"I know."

"Then don't do anything."

Too fucking late.

twenty

KINLEY / Present

THE HORDE of reporters lingering on the sidewalk downstairs has me hiding behind the curtains as I peer down from my bedroom. My once long nails are now uneven ridges from the amount of chewing I've been doing since my phone blew up with texts, voicemails, emails, and social media notifications.

Despite the hotel manager assuring me I'd be fine it didn't make me feel any better. I pace across the hotel room until the carpet is worn by my patterned movements. Free room service is brought to me from management like it's their fault the press is trying to break into the hotel and find me. Every time someone knocks on my door, my muscles lock and panic settles into my bones.

By Saturday night, my agent tells me to stay off social media. My publicist tells me that they're working on taking down comments shared on my online posts, which only makes me itch to see what they're saying. My parents called to ask me what was going on, but I couldn't tell them the truth when I answered. I said things were fine because pretending they are is easier than accepting they're not.

"Kinley, we think it's best you come home sooner rather than later," Jamie Little, from Little's Literary Agency, tells me after the third call of the day.

My time on the film was supposed to last a month. Thirty days to see my imagination come to life before my eyes. Four weeks to experience what it's like to see my dreams come true. In the short time I've been here, I experienced more than that and I'm greedy because I don't want it to end.

Seeing Corbin.

Watching him live his own dream.

We spend so much time holding on to things that make us angry instead of allowing ourselves closure. And for what? It's like we fear who we'll be if we no longer feel the things that we've known for so long. If I hadn't embraced my emotions, I wouldn't have gotten a chance to stand in California at all.

"Kinley?"

I close my eyes. "The media are everywhere, Jamie. I don't see how I could leave right now even if I wanted to."

Her voice is full of surprise. "You don't?"

Is it the movie making me stay or something else? That's what I keep asking myself. Then, like always, I deny what's been just out of reach of my conscience for so long. Acceptance. Admission. I'm glad Jamie told me I was stupid for wanting to pull the plug on the movie when I realized they offered Corbin the lead role. Even on the days when I have to see speculation over him and Lena or hear gossip about him from the people on set, or just watch him play the role so perfectly, I still don't regret coming here.

"This movie means a lot to me."

Jamie never asked why I wanted them to call the whole thing off, but it shouldn't have been hard to guess given what news it followed. She just shook her head and reminded me what it would do for sales. On top of the buzz it was getting from online media outlets, new covers with a movie-based image on the front with Corbin and Olivia would hit shelves right before the movie and double hardcopy sales. She never wanted to ask the reason why because she was like any business-woman out there—in it for the money it'd produce.

At the end of the day, we all had bills to pay. I spent years washing dishes when I didn't want to. I hated the hours, the way my fingers pruned, and how hot the kitchen was. The only thing that made it worth it was the walks and drives home with Corbin, and knowing the money was being saved up to invest in my books.

She's typing something on her computer before answering. "There's a flight I'd like you to be on first thing Monday morning. The press will have cleared out by then, so you'll be able to get to the airport. You'll meet me at my office on Tuesday morning so we can go over what to say to quiet the rumors."

I plop on the end of the bed. "I shouldn't have to make a statement over a fuzzy picture that doesn't mean anything. Won't that just cause more buzz like I'm guilty of something?"

Her sigh is a little reassuring. "You have a point, but we need to discuss it in person. I'm booking your flight. I expect you to be on it."

Leaning my elbows against my bent knees, I rest of forehead in my hand. "I was supposed to have another week and a half here. They're bringing these characters to life, Jamie."

"You have interviews with them," she points out in exasperation. "The entire cast will meet again for a press tour to promote the movie. The premiere party, the red carpet, the talk shows —"

"Put yourself in my shoes," I cut her off.

The benefit of the doubt she gave me before is gone. "I am, Kinley. That's why I'm getting you out of there before this becomes a shit show. We both know you worked too hard for this. There's no need to risk it for a scandal the media are trying to make bank on."

The thing is I can't argue with her. It doesn't matter if she knows the truth or not because it's not her job to deal with the drama in my personal life. She's supposed to sell my books and make sure my image stays clean so we both make money from the work.

"I took you on when you were a teenager and don't regret it one second because you're a hard worker who's dedicated to making something of yourself. Trust me on this. Can you do that?"

The day I walked into her office to go over the contract I'd been offered, I knew I had the option of walking out without putting pen to paper. But Jamie is the exact person I need to help my career move in the direction I want.

"I've trusted you since day one," I admit.

I can picture her smiling. Or her version of smiling, which is the fastest curve of the lips before the movement disappears. It's more like a muscle twitch.

"Monday. Plane."

There's another knock on my door. I walk out of the bedroom and rub a hand down the side of my face. If this hotel offers me another meal without me asking for one, I may blow up. Then I'll spend the rest of the night feeling ten times guiltier over being rude on top of being a pain in their ass along with the other guests impacted by the circus outside.

"I'm not hungry," I tell whoever is standing on the other side, eyeing the peephole.

My eyes widen to twice their size over the dark head of hair peeking out of a hoodie over top of dark sunglasses. I curse and unlock the door, throwing it open in disbelief that I'm seeing the last person who should be here.

"Who's at the door?" Jamie asks.

"Room service," I lie, wincing. "I'll be on the plane. I promise. See you Tuesday morning?"

"My assistant will email you the time."

We say goodbye and I pull Corbin into the room before anyone can see him. That is, if they haven't already. It seems impossible that he walked in without causing a stir.

I end the call and glare at him after making sure the door is locked. "Are you stupid? What the hell are you doing here, Corbin?"

His brows raise. "Good to see you too."

"No. Don't act like I'm being rude," I seethe, walking further into my room. "I'm trying to get those assholes downstairs to leave me alone and stop asking questions about us, and you *show up to my hotel room*?"

B. CELESTE

He keeps his distance and says, "Most of them were escorted off the property before the police were called for disturbance. Plus, I called ahead and got in a different way so nobody would see."

I blink. Then blink again. "And what? I don't believe that nobody saw you. My agent is working to get the rumors circulating about us to go away before something happens. You may be used to this but I'm not. I can't afford to get attacked online for something stupid."

"Stupid?" he repeats.

I ignore his deadpan question. "Why are you here? That's all I want to know, Corbin. I'm leaving sooner than expected and just want to go in peace."

He crosses his arms. "I heard. And I'm here to check in on you. Is that so wrong? We're friends—"

"Stop."

"Don't deny it, Kinley." He walks over to me until his shoes brush the tips of mine. "You can act like there isn't something happening, but then you'd be lying to yourself. You're better than that."

For the first time I think, *am I?*

My silence only feeds his determination to prove what's better left unsaid. "You don't want me here because that means you're willing to truly forgive me. It doesn't matter that you think you already have. Another lie."

"I'm not—"

"I'm sorry," he continues, cutting me off, "for involving you in the shit online. I mean it. You have to understand that I've done everything in my power to try making sure you've been kept out of it for as long as I can."

Does he think I'm stupid? "I'm not proud of admitting this, but I've googled you before. I typed your stupid superstar name into the browser too many times to count. You know what I didn't find? Lincoln. Your family. Me. And I thought … *damn*. He must really hate us. You always said you didn't want to be in Lincoln. How many times did you mention wanting to get out and never look back? So, you did. Only then you deleted that part of your past like it was some blip in the image you wanted to portray."

"That's not—"

"I know," is what I say in a voice far too calm for the conversation. "You can call me a liar and say I'm in denial but I'm just protecting myself. I really thought you deleted that information because you didn't care. It was easier than thinking you did it because you *did* care. That's like admitting that I've always wanted us to find a way back to each other. To touch each other. To hold each other. To say the things we shouldn't say.

"All of those things have been locked away in a vault because they're not worth the pain of acknowledging they can't happen. When I agreed to come to California there were so many different what-if situations running through my head. None of them turned out like this. I told myself to smile and be strong and act like I was better off without you and the memories and everything between us. Do you know what I felt instead?"

His head slowly shakes.

"Sick." His lips part. "Sick like when I worried about messing up our first kiss, or thinking my hand was too sweaty to hold, or wondering if I'd mess up sex and ruin the moment I wanted to share with nobody but you. It's the awkward feeling of trying to play it cool when you're freaking out inside, and trying to decide if the funny feeling in your stomach is butterflies or anxiety, or if the stupid way you smile when you remember something naughty would give you away in front of everybody.

"And *that* is how this will end. I'll touch my lips without thinking about it because I remembered how you kissed me in the trailer and stripped me of my clothes. The public will see because now they've seen us together and they need answers. They'll do anything to put the pieces together even if it means putting them together wrong. Then that smile that teases my lips will disappear when I remember what it felt like to be fucked by you while your *wife* called. Separated or not the vows you said are still valid. Then the feeling in my stomach will weigh me down and all that's left will be guilt. Want to know why, Corbin?"

The tip of his tongue runs across his bottom lip as he gets even closer. His body heat wraps around me like a weighted blanket that holds me down. Except the anxiety of the truth heightens instead of eases.

A tear slips down my cheek. "Because I know that I am so *fucking stupid* for loving you despite it all."

The crack of my voice ends my rant because I know I won't be able to keep talking before I break. Then the only person able to collect the pieces is a man far more broken than me.

A married man.

A former friend.

The end of me.

His hand finds my face, but I find the energy to brush it off. "Do you mean that?"

I part my lips but only manage to shake my head, backing away in retreat. If there was a white flag, I'd wave it. I'd do anything to take back those words and leave them buried inside to suffocate me like they have for over nine years.

A fucking decade I've lied to myself.

I've denied myself the truth.

For what? For this? For him? I don't get a chance to ask because we're suddenly in the same embrace that I've told myself I'm not allowed to be in—the same situation I've insisted on pretending I didn't want.

But I did.

And I do.

And I hate myself more for it than I do him.

When he kisses me, it's cemented.

We're going to hell.

twenty-one

KINLEY / 17

THE AUDITORIUM IS full for the last night of the play, making a permanent smile plaster my face. Closing the corner of the curtain I'm peeking through, I step back into the backstage mayhem as everyone finishes dressing and practicing before it starts in twenty minutes.

Diane, the senior in charge of everything, stops in front of me red-faced and out of breath. She tries speaking but gets nothing out except a raspy breath. The hand clenching her clipboard that people make fun of her for shoots up, her pointer finger gesturing for me to give her a minute to collect herself.

Blinking as she bends over and breathes heavily for a solid fifteen seconds, I glance around looking for Corbin's familiar face. Turns out, so is Diane.

"Where is he?"

"Uh…"

Her eyes widen in horror. "Kinley, where is our leading role? You're always together. You have to know where your boyfriend is."

I eye the clock. Fifteen minutes until showtime. "I'm not sure?" Wincing when she makes a startled noise, I add, "I'm sure he's around here somewhere. He was supposed to be back an hour and a half ago—"

She chokes out, "*Back*?"

Now my nerves are rising. "Everyone knows he started rehearsals for the movie he's in. He goes to the capital region to run lines with everyone before they start shooting next week. He goes a few times a week after school. I'm sure—"

Diane's eyes grow dark. "He signed up for this first! He can't just bail on the last night. What's wrong with him?"

My throat dries. He wouldn't bail on it but telling her wouldn't make much of a difference when she's in freak out mode. I do my best to smile reassuringly, but she storms off yelling for the understudy whose name I don't recognize.

Pulling out my phone, I shoot Corbin a text asking where he is. He kissed me goodbye before leaving last period and said he had a busy afternoon. He made it sound like he'd be back though, and I believe it.

I wait for a response.

When a few minutes go by, everyone in the back starts running around and trying their best to prepare the new lead. I gnaw on my thumbnail and stare between my message app and the time in the righthand corner of my screen.

"Anything?" Diana asks as she flies past me.

All I can do is shake my head.

Corbin wouldn't miss tonight. I know it.

He *promised*.

When I step down from the stage to search the crowd for Zach, who I bribed to come see the last performance in trade of attending his last game, I spot him with a few of his teammates. My feet guide me past peers and families who I try to smile to and wave at like I'm not having a tiny panic attack.

Zach stands up and pulls me in for a tight hug as soon as I get to the end seat he claimed. I manage to hug him back and pull away with a smile that may not look totally pathetic.

"Happy birthday, Kinley."

I roll my eyes. "You already said that today. Three times. And you bought me a Pop Tart from the vending machine."

It was stale, but the thought counted.

He winks. "Just making sure everyone knows. Plus, you hated that Pop Tart. You should have seen your face after the first bite."

Blushing, I brush it off. "Anyway, have you heard from Corbin? Diane is about to have a heart attack because he's not here yet."

He pulls his phone out and glances at it quick. "He hasn't texted me. I wouldn't worry about it, Kin. You know he'll pull through."

My head nods, but I feel a bit of doubt creep into the cracks of my conscious. Guilt follows it, gluing the spaces closed as I wave at him and his buddies. They all start singing happy birthday obnoxiously loud, causing a few confused audience members to join in.

Rushing backstage while they laugh and sing, I do another search of the mass of people lining up and flattening their costumes into perfection. Diane eyes me but must see the helplessness on my face because she focuses on the guy in Corbin's usual costume.

I look at my phone and then shoot him another text, wondering if he's busy driving and unable to text me back. He told me he'd be back by six. It's going on seven now. A hundred different reasons swirl in my head as to why he isn't here. An accident. A blown tire. Maybe he got tied up with the cast.

Someone yells a five-minute warning.

The buzz among the cast as they ask about Corbin

causes Diane to throw her hands up and storm away. The teacher in charge of Drama Club assures everyone that Peter, the understudy, will fill in for Corbin for this performance.

Frowning, I peer back out at the crowd and catch Zach's eye. I shake my head and he does the same and lifts his hands as if to tell me he's sorry for not knowing either. He mouths something but I can't figure out what. Drawing back, I dial Corbin's number and listen to it ring and ring and ring.

It goes to voicemail.

Swallowing, I take a deep breath and remember what he told me at lunch. He would take me out for my birthday after the play. My parents weren't very happy about how late that'd be, but he promised to have me back by eleven thirty. Surprisingly, Gavin got them to agree.

When Zach ran up to me as soon as we got to school and wished me a happy seventeenth birthday, Corbin froze up but smiled and squeezed my hand. It made me wonder if he'd forgotten. As he walked me to home-room like usual, he told me he had my presents at his house that he'd give me when he took me out to celebrate.

I don't blame him for being scatter brained. He's been busy with the play and now the movie, on top of keeping up with school. I help him with homework when we hang out in his rare free time because his mother insisted she'd pull the plug on the movie for him as his legal guardian who signed the contract too. I know how much that would devastate Corbin, so I give him the benefit of the doubt.

When the cast does their normal chant and well wishes for a good play, I defeatedly find my seat in the front row. My phone stays on my lap, screen up, in case he finally gets back to me.

But when the play gets to intermission, there's still nothing to get my hopes up that he'll even make it at all. When I scroll through different social media apps as I wait for the play to continue, I notice Corbin's familiar face with a few others I only recognize because he showed me them in excitement. They're cast members of the movie — some seasoned, some new like him.

It was from thirty minutes ago. They're out to eat. Happy. Laughing.

Standing up and grabbing my coat, I walk up to where Zach's sitting. "I'm heading out. He's not coming."

He sits up straighter. "You heard from him? What's the deal?"

I tap a few buttons and turn the screen toward him to see the picture. "The good news is, he's perfectly fine."

He winces. "Shit. Need a ride?"

I was going to call Gavin but… "Sure. If you don't mind. I really need to get someone to take me to my driver's test so I can finally get my license. I'll have to bribe my brother to do it."

He smacks his friends and says we're leaving, then grabs his things and gestures for me to head toward the back doors. "You okay?"

Shrugging, I give him an unsure smile. "I will be. It's got to be hard for him."

His scoff has me slowing my steps to look at him. "Yeah, dude looked like he's having a miserable time right now."

I sigh. "I meant balancing everything. He's been stressed. His grades haven't been great, so he's trying to get them up that way his mom won't pull him out of the movie—"

"Maybe she should."

My brows furrow. "Should what?"

"Maybe he should quit the movie then."

My head shake is genuine. "He's really good, Zach. What he did tonight sucks for everyone in that auditorium, but you should see him get into character. He loves working on the movie. You can tell he's meant for it."

"What about you?"

I don't say anything.

The cold air hits my face when we swing the doors open and start toward the packed parking lot. "I'm okay. Really. We sort of talked about this kind of thing.

He told me he didn't want me thinking I was being ignored."

Now he's silent.

"He's not ignoring me," I defend. I think about the unanswered texts and calls, clicking my tongue and trying to push the thought away. "I want him to be happy and act."

"Whatever," he grumbles, pulling out his keys and unlocking his car. The blue sedan lights up in the middle of the lot. "You're my friend, Kinley. I just want to make sure you're okay. We could go do something if you want. Get food."

Disappointment settles over me. "I think I'll just head home and get ahead on some homework. Maybe get some writing done."

When we're buckled in, he shifts his body toward me and studies me skeptically. "You're a good person, you know that? Don't let that stop you from raising hell when it's necessary."

I make a face. "It isn't, though."

His eyes tell me, *isn't it?*

THERE'S something hitting my window. When I peel myself up from my toasty sheets, I squint at the time on my alarm and then faceplant back into unconsciousness. Except something hard hits my window again.

Nearly falling off the bed when my foot gets caught

in the throw blanket, I stumble over to the window in question and move the curtain slightly to see what's going on. The streetlight outside illuminates the wet pavement from a steady rain that must have started after I fell asleep around nine.

Mom and Dad thought my plans were cancelled because I was sick. My sluggishness certainly helped my case. Instead of staying up and torturing myself with the story I'm writing about Ryker and Beck, I turned off my phone and slid into bed. I fell asleep watching a documentary on National Geographic.

There's just enough light to see Corbin standing below. He waves his phone around and points to it. I debate on being petty and closing the curtain and curling back in bed. Instead, I turn my phone on and notice the slew of texts and missed calls and voicemails all from him.

His name pops up on the screen again in an oncoming call. My finger hovers over the red decline button, but I want to hear what his excuse is.

"I'm an asshole," he says quickly.

No argument there.

"I swear I didn't forget," he continues. "I kept telling them I had to go, but the entire cast got invited out to get to know each other better since we're going to start filming next week. They reserved a table at some fancy restaurant, and I didn't think I could say no. I'm the youngest and

B. CELESTE

don't want them thinking I have any say when I know I don't."

He speaks so rapidly that he has to suck in deep breath when he's finished. I think about what he says and know it's reasonable. If I were in his shoes I wouldn't want to say no either. Plus, it's good to create a relationship with co-workers to some degree.

"I didn't forget. Promise."

The small breath I inhale eases some of the strain on my lungs. "I understand. But I'm not the only one who you need to apologize to."

His voice is quiet. "I know. Do your parents hate me? They have a right to. Mom told me I'd need to kiss a lot of ass to make this up to you, and—"

"Stop. They think I'm sick."

"They do?"

A tiny smile appears on my face that I'm glad he can't see. "I mean, Gavin has always hated you if that makes a difference…"

He chuckles. "He really does, huh? Hey, I still need to give you your presents. I forgot to put them in my backpack before I left the house, so I couldn't slide them into your locker at school like I planned."

My inner cheek is sucked in by my teeth as I glance at him standing outside. "Can we have a redo? Maybe tomorrow?"

I can't see his smile, but I hear it in the relieved answer he gives me. "I'd love that, Little Bird. Let me

240

make it up to you. I'll pick you up at noon, okay? There will be sugar, presents, and a huge meal that we'll both regret later. I won't even bring up Stephen King."

"I'll believe it when I see it."

Now his laugh is loud and normal, and whatever weirdness was between us is long gone. I move the curtain fully and wiggle my fingers at him before saying goodnight.

When I hang up, a voice clears behind me. Turning around, I see Gavin in his usual black sweatpants and gray tee leaning his shoulder against my doorjamb.

"What are you doing up?" I put my phone back down on the nightstand and settle onto the bed, tucking my feet under the comforter.

"I'm glad I moved the spare key."

My eyes widen. "You really did that?"

His eyes roll like I'm being ridiculous for doubting him. "I wasn't going to let some dude wander into my little sister's room anytime he wanted. I'm just glad he didn't try scaling the tree. Then I'd really have to kick his ass."

I fluff my pillow and rest back. "You wouldn't do that. I like to think you're a giant teddy bear under all those muscles."

He glares like I offended him. "Whatever. Don't wake me up again. And next time the dickhead bails on you, break up with him."

My lips part. "How did you —"

241

He backs up and lifts his hands. "It's a small town, *Little Bird*. We know everything if we ask the right person."

I cross my arms on my chest and pout while he shoots me a wave over his shoulder and wanders back down the hall.

When I pick up my phone, I see a text from Corbin. It's a picture of two wrapped presents—one large and one small. Both with the same silver bow that was on the gift he gave me for Christmas. The paper is blue though, my favorite color. Bright and not dull.

I cuddle into my bed and pull the blanket over me, falling asleep with a smile on my face despite the strangest feeling settling into my stomach.

twenty-two

CORBIN / Present

OUR MOUTHS SLANT over each other's as our tongues battle it out with demanding strokes and breaths. Both my palms hold her face to me like if I let go she'll come to her senses and stop this. It would be the right, rational thing to do.

I don't want to be rational.

Instead, we keep kissing and kissing and breathing each other in like it's our only source of oxygen. Her body pressed against mine, cocooned in my warmth and hardness, makes me want more.

More her.

More this.

More everything.

Backing her up until her ass meets the small table off to the side, I grab her hips and lift her onto it. Her thighs part for me to step between them, our tongues never stopping the dance they're doing. As soon as I'm nestled right where I want to be, I pull her forward so she's on the edge of the wood beneath her. Instinctively, her legs go to either side of my hips and hug them to keep her balanced.

My hands trail down her sides as my mouth travels across her jaw, leaving little bite marks along the way. She catches her breath and writhes as I draw her shirt up and peel it off her completely revealing flawless skin and pert breasts.

"Fuck, baby." My head dips to take one of the hardened buds of her nipples into my mouth and suckle as she bucks forward. Back arching until her chest presses into my face, I lick and suck and nip until her fingers go to my hair and tug hard.

Ignoring her panted pleas, I move to the other nipple and repeat the same movements until she pushes me back. Stumbling, I watch her slide off the table and drop to her knees and fumble with the belt around my waist.

"Kin—" Anything I'm about to say is cut short by the scratchy denim against my thighs as she takes me out and blows on the tip of my engorged head.

I'm choking on air when her mouth wraps around me and a satisfied moan escapes her and vibrates over my cock. My hand goes to the back of her head, fingers weaving into her hair as she takes me in, inch by inch. Her tongue grazes the underside of my length and adds a torturous pressure just below my tip that has me twitching and hardening like steel.

When I cast my eyes downward, I see nothing but chestnut waves bobbing to a rhythm that plays me until my hips meet her every time. My fingers tighten and pull the silky strands in my grasp, causing her to groan again with me deep in her throat.

She withdraws and lets her tongue cast down the side of my cock and back up until her lips wrap around just my head again, putting pressure just below the tip with her lips while swiping her tongue across the precum dripping from me.

Every movement is mastered and skillful, and suddenly my grip on her becomes full of anger and need and so much more. Because what she's doing was fucking taught to her.

But not by me.

Pulling her head back so her lips pop off me, my nostrils flare. "Stand up."

Her eyes widen at the command, but she nods and does as I ask. Before she can say anything, I'm kissing her with a new fervor. My hands go to the back of her thighs and I pick her up until she's wrapped around me.

"Bedroom," is all I say.

She points to the right and I work on suckling her skin and licking the salty taste until her pelvis arches to rub against me.

With a gentleness I didn't know I still had, I lay her on the unmade bed and slowly begin stripping her of her clothes. The pajama pants she's in are plain instead of the colorful ones she used to wear, and the cotton panties are pink, which is a color she never really liked before.

Completely naked, I stare at every inch of her with a heated gaze. Her front teeth dig into her bottom lip as she squirms and tries hiding the rosy nipples that are swollen from my mouth.

She watches with close attentiveness as I strip off my hoodie, then slide out of my jeans. The belt hits the floor like a last warning alarm as my fingers trail under the elastic of my boxers. Her eyes lock on the slowest movement of my fingertips as the last layer between us finds their way to the pile of clothes on the carpet.

The nakedness of the moment is more than just physical as we get our fill of studying every dip, valley, and curve of the other person. We've both seen each other like this before but never with the hunger and distance that settles how we look and act and think now. Her body is curvier, fuller, perkier like she spends time at a gym when she can. Yet there's a softness to her that gives way to a vulnerability I want to take away as she moves her legs to hide the pretty pink pussy I want nothing more than to bury myself in this second.

As I crawl over her on the bed, supporting myself with my arms on either side of her head, she stares up at me with a glassy gaze.

"I hate you," she whispers.

My arms lower, so our bare chests are pressed together. "No. You don't, Little Bird. But you want to."

I kiss her softly, exploring her lips for as long as she'll let me.

She pulls back. "I hate that name."

"No, you don't."

It's her who grazes her mouth against mine, the tip of her tongue tracing the outline of my bottom lip. "I hate who I am with you."

That warrants no response because I know there's truth in that, that seeps a little too deep. So, I let her kiss me, suck my bottom lip into her mouth, and arch her pelvis up to mine until my cock brushes her stomach. We explore in silence and map out every detail that we shouldn't know about each other until we're rolling in the mess of blankets and sheets.

She straddles me. Her palms rest on my chest and she looks down and locks eyes with me. "Do you hate yourself?"

Every single day.

"It would make this easier," she continues, fingers following the indentation of my pec and the slightest smattering of hair lining it. "I wouldn't feel like the bad guy if I knew that I wasn't the only one."

One of my hands covers hers. "You're not the married one, Kinley. I'm the bad guy. I hate myself for what I've done since I stepped out of Lincoln. For choosing my career. For making assumptions. For rushing into marriage. I hate not being able to love you loudly—to hold your hand for everyone to see, to put my hand on your back without the rumors, to kiss you without people criticizing us. I hate myself for doing this wrong, but I hate myself more for dragging you down with me because I need you."

Her eyes close.

"I. *Need*. You," I repeat.

She exhales a breath.

"I. *Love*. You."

A tear sticks to her eyelashes.

"And I've never stopped."

She bends down and presses her chest against mine, sending racks of shivers down my spine from the contact. We kiss. We cry. We breathe. And in the slowest, gentlest fashion possible, I flip us over and guide myself inside her until I'm seated fully.

I think about the past and kiss her.

I think about the present and caress her.

I think about the future and hold her.

But the cool depths of reality tell us that this moment is temporary, so we make the most of the weight and warmth and the need that our bodies crave. I vibrate with it so brutally as I slowly enter her again and again.

The softest exhale of my name from her parted lips as I take my time with her has me swelling. She wraps her legs around me, and angles herself up so I'm further in. We both moan as we find our pace, my body coming down completely on hers, and pushing as deep as I can until there's no clear indication of who is who.

Her fingernails rake down my naked back, digging in with a pain that I welcome. I want her to mark my flesh and engrave herself into my existence for good.

Because I meant what I said.

I need her.

I need her fast wit and sarcasm.

I need every emotion — good and bad.

I need the feeling that has cemented itself so concretely in my chest that tells me how stupid I was when I was eighteen. So fucking stupid. I need it all, even if it destroys me and what I've built for myself because nothing compares.

So, I breathe the words over and over again, punctuating each one with the deepest thrust that brings us closer to the edge.

"I need you."

The bed creaks.

"I need you."

Her breath catches.

"I need you."

Her nails pierce my skin.

My hips move into a circle, grinding down on her until she's making the noise that is music to my ears. She tightens around me with every push, and the kisses I land on her chest, collarbone, neck, and lips all bring her closer and closer.

Yet, nothing quickens my pace.

This isn't screwing or fucking or a one-time thing between people who don't care. We're consumed and that's the problem. We care too much.

I make love to her slowly, finding her hands and intertwining our fingers because I need this—the contact, the warmth, the empty promise that rests openly between us. Once it's over, then everything we've been through is final.

It's over.

It ends.

And no matter how many highs we chase to find the feeling that's stayed between us since the day I stepped foot into Lincoln, nothing can mimic it. The flutters. The spark. The restlessness.

When our tongues meet and our bodies jerk and our breaths mix, there's no stopping from the climax that takes over us. Her hands let go of mine no matter how badly I want her to hold on, and she wraps herself around me in a tight hug as she milks my cock of cum.

Even after the tremors end, after our breathing

evens, we stay like that. Wrapped up in a fantasy world like we can stay. The truth is there in the bunched sheets and scattered clothes.

This time, she'll leave.

Resting in silence with nothing but traffic sounding in the distance, she traces my chest. Her fingers go to the very spots where two little lines used to be. She stills when she notices the slightly lifted ridge of a third one.

She sits up, staring at my chest.

Three tally marks.

"Corbin?"

I swallow, finding her hand. "I wasn't completely honest with you about the tattoos. I do think we're equal, that we're meant to take on the world like nobody else. But these lines are so much more than that."

The emotion on her face goes to her eyes, glazing them with oncoming tears. I want to brush them away, kiss her in comfort, protect her from the pain.

"Each line represents the moment I realized I loved you," I admit, tracing the first one closest to my heart. "When you fell asleep next to Fred after helping me run lines." My finger finds the middle line. "When you got me that audition for Christmas, one that neither of us knew at the time would change my life." I move along to the newest one. "When I saw you walk onto set, looking so fucking beautiful it hurt. I knew,

Kinley. I knew that my Little Bird would always be mine."

Her lashes bat away stray tears, some catching in them until she wipes them away. "I don't know what to say, Corbin. I'm…"

I pull her into me, hugging her warm body to mine and trying to make the moment last. I know it won't. "Don't say anything. Just let me hold you for a little while longer, okay?"

She doesn't argue.

My Little Bird stays.

twenty-three

CORBIN / Present

EXTRA SECURITY IS PLACED on set and nobody is being let in without clearance first. It's been two days since the pictures surfaced, so the media has died down enough to keep working. The absence of Kinley on set doesn't go unnoticed though.

Bright and early Monday morning, Buchannan made the announcement that Kinley had to go back to New York. Despite the few weeks she spent with us, it's obvious she made an impact. She always made an effort to talk with everyone on set, no matter what position they held. It was never just to get away from me, though I'm sure that was an added bonus on her part, but because she cared.

I step foot in the final scene before lunch, where Olivia is perched on the counter. Her long legs dangle over the side, and she's only in an oversized button down white shirt with a few buttons keeping her from being completely exposed. She shoots me a wink when I situate myself where I'm supposed to be.

"So ... Kinley, huh?"

From the corner of my eye, I notice Buchannan direct a few of the cameramen as to how he wants the scenes shot. "Not now, Liv. I don't want to talk about it."

Her shoulders lift as she leans back, supporting herself with her hands. "Hey, why didn't the cow read the book?" Her eyebrows wiggle at me right before she delivers the punchline. "He was waiting for the moo-vie."

Her cackle just has me rolling my eyes, causing her to straighten and sigh. "Get it? Because Kinley wrote the book and we're in the movie and you both came from the middle of—"

"Stop," I warn under my breath. It isn't often I let my anger get out when I speak to co-workers, but she knows I spent a lot of time and money to get the press to stay out of my business when it came to Lincoln.

She groans. "You do realize that people around here are going to find out, right? Those pictures of you two are only the first step. You know how this works. They'll move on to the next big thing and circle back to speculation once you're out and about looking mopey like your puppy ran away."

My eyes cut to her. "There's nothing for them to — "

"Nope."

"Kinley is just — "

"Try again." She inspects her nails. "You don't want to accept that things will change, do you? They already have, Callum. Or can I call your Corbin?"

I don't say anything.

Her legs swing in a slow, causal movement. "She didn't look at you the way she did when she first came here if that means anything to you. And I think it does."

Again, nothing.

"Kind of ironic, really."

This gets my attention. "What is?"

"She left before she could see what happens between Beck and Ryker play out. It's almost like she never got closure..."

Again, is what she doesn't say.

And fuck me, if Olivia isn't perceptive. Not to mention *right*. Kinley wrote a story that was based on us, whether she admits it or not, and just like how I fucked up the first time, we're screwed over again from our ending. I told her we'd keep in touch this time — that it would be different because we're older and have control over what we choose to do with our lives. All she did was ask me to leave her hotel room.

Her voice had broken as she watched me open the door, and said, *"Don't make promises you can't keep, Corbin. We've been down that road before."*

I never assured her it would be different because I knew there was no point. Her eyes were full of doubt and unspoken emotion and her arms hugged her chest like she was the only person who could comfort herself.

So, I stepped into the hallway, glanced over my shoulder, and told her, *"We're inevitable, Little Bird."*

Though her expression didn't seem so sure, I knew she felt it. Why else would we fall back into old patterns so easily? It's because we don't want to miss out on the feeling that connected us since we were young and stupid.

"What are you thinking about?" Olivia asks, her legs stilling.

"Nothing," I lie, picking a piece of lint off my shirt and rolling my shoulders back.

"Liar."

I simply shrug.

Buchannan walks over to us. "You two ready? We'll be finishing your scenes together today and tomorrow and do any reshoots necessary the rest of the week before moving on to the last minute stuff."

We both nod and take our places.

Olivia starts the scene as soon as we're told the

cameras are rolling. One of her legs drifts up, the shirt exposing the bottom of her pert ass as I lean forward against the counter and watch her lazily.

Her fingers trail up her leg. "Do you think it would have been like this if we'd given in to each other all those years ago?"

I straighten and make my way around the island, trapping her on the counter between my arms. Her legs part and easily wrap around me, her arms draping themselves on my shoulders. Flashbacks of my night with Kinley replay in my mind, fogging the lines that I know I need to deliver.

Olivia eyes me subtly.

I raise my hand to her cheek, moving a piece of hair out of her face and curling it behind her ear using my knuckles. "I think we wouldn't be sure about each other if there wasn't pain to fight through. How would we know this is worth fighting for if there wasn't a battle to face?"

She leans into my touch. "How will we know if we survive it? Battles turn into wars, Ryker. Not everyone survives."

Her hands trail down my sides until they bunch the shirt I'm wearing. I watch her like I'd watch Kinley, with fascination over everything she does. The way her eyes skirt over my face, how her warmth absorbs into my skin through the expensive material of my dress shirt. I picture chestnut hair and fair skin and big brown eyes in front of me, and it makes me feel every-thing Ryker does for Beck.

"We'll be the exception," I tell her with a conviction I wish I delivered to Kinley when we parted ways. "Some people don't survive because they're too busy looking over their shoulder. We have each other."

"You really believe that?"

Both my hands move to her face. "I believe that the reason I never let you go was because I was waiting for a second chance. This is it, Little Bird. It's now or never."

Realizing my mistake as soon as the nickname escapes my mouth, I play it out. Olivia does the same, slightly startled but willing to go along with it.

Her mouth ascends on mine, claiming my lips in a kiss that only two people who are beautifully broken can understand. There's an understanding between us that our kiss explains silently with every brush, suck, and breath. I try channeling Ryker the best I can, grip-ping her sides and making her mine like I've always wanted. Yet the surge of emotion that I feel coursing through my veins with my actual Little Bird is absent. Ryker will never let Beck go because he thinks this is their last shot—this moment cements what he's always wanted. Needed.

When Buchannan calls cut, I instantly back up and wait for the scolding over ruining the scene with my botched lines. But when I turn and see everyone staring at me, there's awe on their faces instead.

Buchannan walks over to me and puts his hand on my shoulder, squeezing. "I don't know what that was, but there's not one person in this room that didn't feel it. Damn, kid. And the Little Bird bit —"

I rush out an apology. "I'm sorry about that. It just slipped out. If we need to redo the scene, I understand."

"Redo it?" Buchannan shakes his head. "I worked with you back when you were what? Nineteen? Twenty? You were just starting and there was passion since day one, but what you just did exceeds anything I've seen you do. You're a good actor, but great ones channel their emotions into the job. I don't know what significance Little Bird is to you, but I'm keeping it in the scene. Beck deserves to have a nickname."

He squeezes my shoulder again before walking away and nodding at something somebody tells him along the way. Panic builds in the pit of my stomach as I swipe a hand through my styled hair and messing up the perfectly placed strands.

"Oh my God," Olivia whispers. "You really love her, don't you?"

I turn ever so slowly.

She blinks. "You are so fucked."

Twenty-four

KINLEY / Present

THE FAMILIARITY of being back in my territory has me walking a little lighter and waving to people with a soft smile on my face. The tightness in my chest disappeared as soon as I walked into my home and saw Penny, short for Pennywise—my calico cat, run towards me. I know my neighbor took good care of her, but I still missed being the one to watch her gobble treats and demand attention at the most inconvenient times.

Since I've been back, I've thrown myself into work to complete my newest project and stay up to date with Jamie and the team following our meeting. Jamie

Little is a five-foot-five intimidating woman who's always ready for anything. There's rarely a smile on her serious face, which screams success in how she carries herself. Her styled white bob never moves an inch out of place and her wardrobe probably costs more than I make in a year. But that's why I love her. She's the perfect woman to conduct business in a no-nonsense way.

The three weeks that I've been back have been a whirlwind of edits, meetings, and local promotional tours. Jamie's literary agency works hand in hand with a publicist who helps me keep my social media regulated since the media raised questions regarding me and Corbin, but since there's been nothing since about us, things have gone as smoothly as possible.

After a book signing at a store twenty minutes from my little townhome, I come home to a wrapped package in my mailbox. When I pull it out with the rest of the bills and assorted mail, my lips part at what I'm seeing.

A rectangular package.

A silver bow.

Staring at the slightly torn blue wrapping paper, I brush the pad of my thumb across the hard item under it. Déjà vu hits me as I distractedly walk into my house.

Penny jumps on the couch where I sit down, nudging the gift that rests on my lap. Her purrs pull me away from the unknown just inches away. I rub between her ears and listen to her rumbles grow louder, finding myself smiling at the ball of fluffy love sniffing the mail.

The label on the back tells me what I already know, but my eyes don't stray from the name regardless. I've received many things from California, but never from him. His name is the last thing I expect to cross while going through my private mail.

Penny paws the bow, tearing one of the sides with her claw. "No, Pen." Part of me debates on giving in and letting her have it, but another remembers the few others identical to it that rest in a box in my office.

Swallowing past an emotion that I've been trying hard to avoid since boarding the plane at LAX airport, I begin tearing open the paper until something black with gold lettering is revealed underneath.

I blink down at the *Girl Boss* notebook with golden edges. My fingers run down the cover, tracing the small words in utter silence.

Penny yowls.

I notice something else in the package, trapped in the wrapping paper I tore. Pulling out a piece of paper, I study the two words written in familiar handwriting that covers hotel stationary.

Open it.

Hesitantly, I lift the notebook and peel open the cover. The soft crack of a new spine greets my ears. Eyes scanning the pages in front of me, I notice more of the same black handwritten words written on the inside of the cover.

A blank notebook for the start of something new, because our story isn't over yet.
Fly with me, Little Bird.
~ Corbin

BLINKING back tears as my eyes dance across the phone number he also provided below, I close the book and set it on the table with the other mail I've yet to pay attention to. Penny nudges my thigh as I sit in the silence and just look at the present. How did he even get my address? Questions swirl around my head, leaving my gaze blurry and my stomach twisting.

He signed it Corbin, not Ryker. There's a significance to that. Like even though the character he portrays gets his happy ending, Corbin isn't willing to settle. But he has to. Can't he see that? Unless something changes, there won't be anything more to the story he's so determined I write a continuation to.

Just last week, pictures of Corbin and Lena surfaced in front of the bluest ocean I've never had the opportunity to see. The article had to mention the images of me and him at the drugstore, making light on how their marriage is strong despite the rumors. And as much as I wanted to throw my phone when I saw them plastered on my newsfeed, I know what a genuine smile from Corbin looks like. The one spread on his face in each picture taken by who knows is fake.

And I'm sick for being happy about it.

Brushing off the image of his arm around his wife's bare waist in her tiny bikini, I stand and forget about what rests on the coffee table. If I were smart, I'd throw it away or stick it in the box with my other notebooks.

I'm not smart though.

Walking into the kitchen and digging through my stash of candy on the counter, I greedily rip open the package of Twizzlers and bite down onto one. As I make my way to the home office set up by my bedroom, my face scrunches at the sudden nausea sweeping through my system. Staring down at the strand of licorice that's almost gone only makes it worse. Before I know what's happening, I'm diving toward the white wastebasket positioned by my large desk.

The sweet smell of artificial sugar scattered on my laptop by my face causes me to lurch more into the bucket. My knees dig into the carpet as I kneel help-lessly on the floor. The burn of my throat makes my eyes water as I come up for air, gagging over the horrid smell of vomit.

Penny stands by the door, tail twitching, watching me with a cocked head. When the sugary smell that I usually indulge in hits my nose again, I grab the candy and throw it into the hall far away from me. Offended, Penny darts into our room.

Resting my forehead against the edge of my desk for a moment, I force myself up and toward the bathroom attached to my bedroom. Cleaning out the waste basket, I set it on the floor and then splash cold water on my face. When I examine myself in the mirror, I'm greeted with flushed cheeks and red eyes.

Shaking my head, I rinse out my mouth and brush my teeth to get rid of the putrid taste that's lingering. When I grab a towel to dab my mouth, I notice something sticking out of the vanity cabinet below.

Mouth gaping, I shake my head to myself and begin counting back in my head. Penny's demanding yowls are drowned out by the math I'm trying to do mentally. Panic courses through me as I plop down on the closed toilet seat and stare at the tile floor.

Choking on air, I whisper, "No."

Twenty-five

KINLEY / Present

MY FINGERS TIGHTEN around the Celebrity Access magazine, crinkling the flimsy cardstock-like cover until the familiar image of America's Most Desired Man is as flawed as the headline. It's the signature side smirk teasing a narrow slit of perfectly white teeth and a deep dimple in the dark stubble patch of his cheek that makes everyone pick up the latest edition. The brazen silver eyes framed with dark lashes against clear olive skin is almost as deadly as the charming wink he shoots to the cameras.

Corbin Callum oozes the kind of sex appeal that

could get him out of anything. It's proven by the bolded white headline hanging over his unkempt black hair. Messy in a I-spend-an-hour-achieving-this-look kind of way. Gelled but not too gelled. Unruly but not too unruly. They portray him as anything but a cheater. A *rumored* cheater. An adulterer.

My free hand goes to my stomach, the feel of my cotton purple tunic soft beneath my touch. What's not soft is the rounded skin underneath the layer of clothing. It's new. Always changing. A reminder.

The headline doesn't give away the feminine name now attached to his, but the article doesn't shy away from using it eight times in the three-column exposé. A grainy picture of a chestnut-haired woman smiling too wide, standing too close, and angled too intimately saddles the accusation. They say a picture is worth a thousand words.

My hand twitches.

The picture they're bound to get in just over seven more months will be worth even more.

Corbin Callum rumored to be involved with bestselling author on set of his latest movie. Pictures inside.

I close my eyes and absorb the heavier pitter-patter of droplets of rain outside the window of my master bedroom. My grip of the magazine loosens until it hits the carpeted floor with a soft thud. I do nothing about the bent pages despite the money I spent.

I remember it all—the way our lips sounded when

they tasted each other's. How our teeth clashed in desperation and our hands roamed with urgency. The ghost sting of pulled hair and rewarded groans linger in my awareness, branded with a scorching steal rod in the front of my mind. Gentle lips against a ticklish throat. Wandering fingertips against sensitive flesh.

He was there.

Everywhere.

Taking. Giving. Offering. Sacrificing.

Remember, Little Bird?

Remember what it felt like?

Exhaling shakily, I open my eyes and stare down at the ultimate plot twist in a story that's taken nine years to develop. Nostrils twitching with oncoming emotion, I lick my chapped lips and let the metallic taste bring me back to reality.

"I remember," I choke out, curling up on my side and cradling my barely-there stomach, all while wondering if the baby will have his eyes or mine.

My agent calls.

I let it go to voicemail.

To be continued in *Where the Little Birds Are...*

acknowledgments

Where the Little Birds Go was created from a Screen-writing course I took in grad school. The urge to write a Hollywood Romance was one I couldn't ignore after proposing the story to my professor, so I opted to expand it from a screenplay to a full-length novel. Then I thought ... why not two? Thus, the Little Birds duet was born.

I first want to shoutout my Momager, Micalea Smeltzer, for always supporting me and telling me what to do because I continue to forget how to adult. I love you, Kris.

To my betas Jessica, Alicia, Micalea, and Melissa, you

ladies always help me better my books and I am so thankful to have you in my corner.

Thanks to my PA Jessica for running my groups so I could shut myself away and get this book written. You are a Godsend.

These gorgeous covers are all thanks to Letitia Hasser from RBA Designs. She has brought all my books to life with her amazing talent and brilliant imagination and I cannot be more proud to have such breathtaking, original covers to represent my stories.

The beautiful teasers are all thanks to Emily Wittig who I could not be more thankful for, for helping me create something gorgeous when I had no time between school, work, and writing.

It always takes a village to make books happen, and I am thankful for every single person who takes a chance on me and my stories. Thank you to the readers for all you've done and continue to do to make this dream a reality.

Until book two,
    B. Celeste

about the author

B. Celeste's obsession with all things forbidden and taboo enabled her to pave a path into a new world of raw, real, emotional romance.

Her debut novel is The Truth about Heartbreak.

Made in the USA
San Bernardino, CA
17 February 2020